Stories from The Edge

by

Bryony Pearce

Paula Rawsthorne

Dave Cousins

Sara Grant

Katie Dale

Savita Kalhan

Miriam Halahmy

Keren David

Albury Books

Teen Books from Edge authors

If you like the stories in this anthology, you might enjoy these books from The Edge authors:

Bryony Pearce
Angel's Fury
The Weight of Souls
Phoenix Rising
Phoenix Burning
Windrunner's Daughter
Wavefunction

Paula Rawsthorne
The Truth About Celia Frost
Blood Tracks

Dave Cousins
15 Days without a Head
Waiting for Gonzo

Sara Grant
Dark Parties
Half Lives
Chasing Danger

Katie Dale
Someone Else's Life
Little White Lies

Savita Kalhan
The Long Weekend

Miriam Halahmy
Hidden
Illegal
Stuffed
The Emergency Zoo

Keren David
When I Was Joe
Almost True
Another Life
Lia's Guide to Winning the Lottery
Salvage
This is Not a Love Story
Cuckoo

First published in 2016 by Albury Books
Albury Court, Albury,
Thame, Oxfordshire, OX9 2LP

www.alburybooks.com

Cover Design by En Tsao

A CIP catalogue record for this title is available from the British Library

Printed and bound by CPI Group (UK) Ltd, Croydon, CR0 4YY

ISBN 978-1-910571-60-6

Stories from The Edge

by

Bryony Pearce

Paula Rawsthorne

Dave Cousins

Sara Grant

Katie Dale

Savita Kalhan

Miriam Halahmy

Keren David

CONTENTS

Welcome to The Edge

Introduction   p1

Face2Face – Bryony Pearce   p3
Alex has been searching for a year – searching online for the one guy who ticks all the right boxes. She knows exactly what she's looking for . . . But then so does he!

A Level Playing Field – Paula Rawsthorne   p24
Seventeen-year-old Alfie Pickford has sacrificed so much in his quest to become a world-class swimmer, but as he competes in the most important race of his life, has Alfie pushed himself too far this time?

Magpie Soup – Dave Cousins   p39
It's Mum's funeral today. Dad's completely lost the plot and just tried to go out without his trousers on. It wasn't supposed to be like this. Mum didn't want a house full of sad people trying not to cry. Which is why I made some alternative arrangements of my own. . .

Nightlight – Sara Grant   p51
Regret is keeping Helen Friar up tonight. The events of the afternoon haunt her. If she could erase today and try it again, she would. But there are no do-overs in real life.

Trick or Tweet? – Katie Dale   p55

Now's my chance. I can do this. I've been planning it long enough. By following Chloe's Twitter-feed I've discovered all her likes, her dislikes – even where she lives. I know @Chlover better than any girl I've ever met. Though we've never actually met.
But at tonight's Halloween party all that's about to change. . .

Aladdin's Lamp – Savita Kalhan   p68

Priti wishes she had an Aladdin's Lamp.
She would wish for all her suitors to go away.
She would wish for her best friend to stay in India.
But Priti finds out that you have to be careful what you wish for. . .

Next Stop, the Eiffel Tower – Miriam Halahmy   p83

Fifteen-year-old Madi is hoping to meet hot French boys on a visit to a Paris school with her author mum. Sure enough, gorgeous Jean Luc invites her out with his friends. But when they skip school the next morning, the streets suddenly turn into terror. Madi survives but will she ever recover?

The Day I Told the Truth – Keren David   p99

Ethan's parents live in different countries, and don't speak much – and after their bitter divorce, that's the way Ethan likes it. But now they are all going to dinner together. Is it time for Ethan to tell them the truth?

About the Authors   p115

Acknowledgements

Welcome to The Edge

We are a group of award-winning, UK-based authors, writing sharp fiction for young adults and teens. Together we have more than fifty books published in twenty countries around the world. We are thrilled to present our first anthology.

Stories from The Edge is a collection of gripping tales with teenagers at their heart. These stories pack a powerful punch, covering a wide range of issues and ideas that we hope will not only entertain, but also make readers think. Discussion guides for exploring each of the stories with students are available as a free download from our website: **http://edgeauthors.blogspot.co.uk**

Formed in early 2011, The Edge started with a shared blog to create a focus point for discussion about books for young people. We have always been interested in providing a platform for readers, librarians, booksellers and bloggers to share their thoughts and experiences. Most of all, we love taking The Edge into schools and hearing what young people think. The Edge offers workshops, readings, talks and panel discussions in person, or via Skype. Our books, events and activities are suitable for readers from Year 7 to adult.

You can read more about us and our books in the 'About the Authors' section at the back of the anthology.

For more information or to discuss a booking:
Email: edgewriters@yahoo.co.uk
Website: Keep up to date with the latest Edge activities and news at
http://edgeauthors.blogspot.co.uk
Follow us on **Twitter:** @EdgeWriters
Or YouTube: www.youtube.com/user/EdgeAuthorsTV

Thanks for joining us. We hope you enjoy our stories from The Edge.

INTRODUCTION

If you are a teenager browsing the bookshelves, why would you care what I think? But I challenge you to read the first story in this collection – it really won't take long. Good? And the great thing about anthologies? Every story is completely different. I read thousands of books a year (great job, eh?), so you can trust me when I promise that you will definitely not be bored!

Teachers and librarians wondering about spending your budget? This is for you: The short story is a very powerful weapon in the hands of a librarian or teacher trying to get young people hopelessly addicted to reading. As a lifelong addict myself I know what I am talking about! They are the perfect length for reading aloud, and listening to a story is a pleasure none of us ever grow out of. These stories will certainly hold the attention of any group of teenagers! They are also the perfect length to use in lessons to study the craft of writing. In the hands of a skilled writer just a few pages can envelop you in a different world, engage you in a character's life and dilemmas, thrill, chill, make you laugh or cry.

Certainly *Stories from The Edge* can do all of those things in spades! The Edge authors are some of the most exciting writers in the thriving UK teen market. Between them they have a substantial body of published work so this anthology is also a great way to introduce young people to their next favourite author. I guarantee that these stories will leave them gasping for more. But most importantly they will get teen readers thinking and talking. From the perils of online chat rooms, doping in sport, racism and terrorism, to gender and self-esteem issues, love, life and death, we run the full gamut of teenage concerns in this volume.

We 'gatekeepers' know that one of the most important reasons for reading stories is building empathy and understanding, and it is the conversations springing from a shared reading which can be the most productive of results. An added bonus for this anthology is some really excellent discussion guides for each story which can be downloaded from http://edgeauthors.blogspot.co.uk. The blog is a great one to bookmark too – there's always something interesting to read. But don't stop at this online contact! The other key feature of The Edge authors is that they love to meet and work with young people. (That is how their teenage voices and characters so consistently ring true.) Get them into your school – I guarantee you won't regret it. You won't regret buying this anthology either. In fact, how about a set for your class?

Joy Court
Chair: CILIP Carnegie & Kate Greenaway Medals;
Reviews Editor: *The School Librarian*

FACE2FACE

by Bryony Pearce

Chatz

LilMissSunshine: Anyone out there wanna chat?

Kpat25: Cute pic. U in the UK?

LilMissSunshine: Nr London. U?

KPat25: Canada. Y up so late?

. . .

Kpat25: Where R U? Thought U wanted to chat?

Friends online

LilMissSunshine: Anyone out there wanna chat?

Demon300: I'm up for it, if U R.

LilMissSunshine: U mean chatting, right?

Demon300: U look sexi. Wanna see a pic of me?

LilMissSunshine: Can see ur pic, thx.

Demon300: Not that pic, this one. . .

. . .

Demon300: Don't be a prude.

. . .

Demon300: Bitch.

Face2Face

LilMissSunshine: Anyone out there wanna chat?

Nate31: Hey. R U up late, or R U outside UK?

LilMissSunshine: Up late. U?

Nate31: Same. Big test TMRW. Revising.

LilMissSunshine: Me 2! Just finished. Can't sleep. Wotz urs?

Nate31: Biology module. Urs?

LilMissSunshine: AS English. Yuck.

Nate31: Tread softly because you tread upon my dreams.

LilMissSunshine: Yeats, right?

Nate31: Maybe. It's the only quote I know. Stepbitch has it on her fridge.

LilMissSunshine: As U do!

Nate31: Exactly. Do U get on with ur parents?

LilMissSunshine: Not really. It's as if they live in another century. They'd go nuts if they knew I was on Face2Face this time of night. Like the only way to communicate is in person, as if that's how U meet interesting people. They're all, be careful on the Internet, don't give away any personal details. Like there're a million paedos out there just waiting to pounce on me if I go online!

Nate31: Right. Because only people who want to kidnap U and sell U into slavery go online.

LilMissSunshine: LOL ☺

Nate31: But seriously, what if ur soulmate was like a hundred miles away or something, how do U meet them if U don't go online?

LilMissSunshine: U believe in soulmates?

Nate31: Don't U?

LilMissSunshine: Makes it sound like there's only one person for everyone. That's sad ☹.

Nate31: U could have more than one soulmate. Maybe mate is the wrong word, it sounds like marriage ☺. Maybe I mean soul friends. People who just GET U, y'know.

LilMissSunshine: Yeah, like ur circle. What if the people u're meant to hang with just live somewhere else?

Nate31: Exactly.

LilMissSunshine: We're lucky – we can meet each other online. Maybe ur olds are bitter.

Nate31: Poor friendless parents.

LilMissSunshine: Hang on, BRB

. . .

LilMissSunshine: Parental check up. Lights out.

Nate31: U under the covers now?

LilMissSunshine: That how U do it?

Nate31: No need. Stepmum – she lets me do whatever.

LilMissSunshine: I'm hiding, but should go to sleep really – test 2morrow.

Nate31: Good luck.

LilMissSunshine: U 2. GLHF

Nate31: Wanna chat TMRW?

LilMissSunshine: I'll poke U.

You have a new text message

Ellie: How late were U up last night?

Alex: Late. U?

Ellie: Watched some TV. Listened to some music. Skyped with SkaterBoy.

Alex: So things R going well there?

Ellie: GR8! Were U on chat rooms again?

Alex: Yes. Ellie . . . I reckon I might've found him this time.

Ellie: You've thought so B4.

Alex: This time I'm sure.

Ellie: You've been trying for almost a year. If this isn't him, will U give up?

Alex: Maybe.

Ellie: U shld move on.

Alex: U sound like Dr Tedious.
Ellie: LMBO. How's ur mum?
Alex: The same.
Ellie: R U going to tell her?
Alex: God, no. C U @ school?
Ellie: Obvs.

Face2Face
To Nate31: LilMissSunshine has poked you.
To LilMissSunshine: Nate31 has poked you back.
LilMissSunshine: Hey. How was the test?
Nate31: Nightmare. Urs??
LilMissSunshine: Misspelled Coriolaynis all the way through . . .
bugger, did it again.
Nate31: ROFL
LilMissSunshine: Wht else U do 2day? Wht U into?
Nate31: SSDD. But I got in a hockey match after school. Suppose U
don't like hockey?
LilMissSunshine: ORLY? Cos I'm a girl.
Nate31: Not many people into it.
LilMissSunshine: If its ur thing, it's cool.
Nate31: I play for the county. Kind of a BFD on the pitch.
LilMissSunshine: Not to brag.
Nate31: Or anything.
LilMissSunshine: So U had practice 2day?
Nate31: After school. Went well. Scored a couple of goals. What
about U, what U into?
LilMissSunshine: Art's my thing.
Nate31: Painting n drawing?
LilMissSunshine: Sculpture. We've got our own wheel n I do a lot
with wire. Whatevr, U don't want to know. . ..
Nate31: I do actually. Got any pics of ur stuff?

LilMissSunshine: U really interested?

Nate31: Sure. It's a window into ur soul.

LilMissSunshine: There U go again with souls. LOL. U religious?

Nate31: Not really. Just my own brand of spiritualism. I believe in karma. Don't U?

LilMissSunshine: U mean what goes around, comes around? Yeah, I do actually.

Nate31: So – U got any pics?

LilMissSunshine: None without me in them making goofy faces. Not sure they're for the public.

Nate31: No public. Only me. PLS

LilMissSunshine: Still not sure. . .

Nate31: I promise not to laugh.

LilMissSunshine: OK. FYEO

Attachment

. . .

LilMissSunshine: Wht R U thinking?

Nate31: That's amazing. Wot is it?

LilMissSunshine: Cheers!

Nate31: Kidding. Obvs flowers. Wire flowers. But they're dying, right? Dying wire flowers.

LilMissSunshine: Now U think I'm weird.

Nate31: Nah. Cool. Subversive.

LilMissSunshine: Subversive. Y?

Nate31: U have a life n death thing, right? Juxtapositions.

LilMissSunshine: OMG. U really get it!

Nate31: Something about U in that pic. You look somehow familiar.

LilMissSunshine: Maybe we've met in real life? That would be crazy.

Nate31: Don't think so. I'd remember U for sure. Those gorgeous eyes!

LilMissSunshine: Blush

Nate31: SRSLY. Gotta go right now. Poke U l8r?

LilMissSunshine: Out 2nite. Spk tmrw?

You have a new text message

Alex: It's him. The one I've been waiting for.

Ellie: How do U know?

Alex: He's into hockey. Plays for the county.

Ellie: People do, U know

Alex: Biology A level.

Ellie: So, he's our age.

Alex: He keeps going on about souls, soulmates. He's THE ONE.

Ellie: Don't move too fast. Think.

Alex: I am thinking. I'm thinking he's the one.

Face2Face

To LilMissSunshine: Nate31 has poked you.

Nate31: R U there, Miss Sunshine?

. . .

LilMissSunshine: Sorry, late tea.

Nate31: Anything nice?

LilMissSunshine: Mum's a decent cook, actually. Lasagne. God I'm boring. What R U up to?

Nate31: SSDD. Missing U. Wishing we could talk more.

LilMissSunshine: Really?

Nate31: My school is filled with these shallow losers. You're not like other girls. You're so much more than just make up and boy bands. You're interesting to talk to. Your art is something real. I can't believe I don't even know your name!

LilMissSunshine: I don't know urs either.

Nate31: It's Nate, LOL. Assuming U aren't called Sunshine, though . . .

LilMissSunshine: ☺ Mum won't let me use my real name on my profile. She's a Nazi.

Nate31: So what is it? Bet it's really pretty, like U.

LilMissSunshine: U'll be disappointed then. Maybe we'll stick with Sunshine for now.

Nate31: If you insist, Sunshine. LOL

LilMissSunshine: Played hockey today?

Nate31: Every day. Gotta practise if I want to keep my place in the county team.

LilMissSunshine: Bet u're really good.

Nate31: Yeah. Gotta practise, though. I guess u're the same with your art, I bet U work at it every spare minute so you can get better and better. Can't get rusty. Does ur school do hockey?

LilMissSunshine: In the winter, athletics ATM.

Nate31: Bet u're good. U look like U look after urself.

LilMissSunshine: Not really. Dreaded hurdles this week, almost broke an ankle. I'm better at javelin, discus and that. I've got strong arms.

Nate31: From working with wire and stuff?

LilMissSunshine: Maybe. OMG, U did not need to know that.

Nate31: I so did. Bet U have to wear those cute little skirts too. Our lot wear blue. What colours urs?

LilMissSunshine: Hideous red. We all look like Velma.

Nate31: Scooby Doo? ROFL. Mental image of Velma throwing javelin at Shaggy and Scooby. Hang on, Stepbitch is yelling. Gotta take out the bins. BRB.

. . .

I'm back. Bloody bin night. So . . . that got me thinking.

LilMissSunshine: About rubbish?

Nate31: That too, LOL. I've got a problem and I thought maybe you could help. I can talk to U can't I?

LilMissSunshine: Sure.

Nate31: I already feel like I can talk to U about anything.

LilMissSunshine: Is this the soulmate thing again?

. . .

Nate?

Nate31: Maybe I'll just leave it for now. We can talk again tmrw.

LilMissSunshine: I didn't mean to upset U.

Nate31: It's OK. It's late. School in the morning.

LilMissSunshine: Don't go. Tell me ur problem. I'm a good listener.

. . .

Nate, RUOK?

Nate31: I'm not great at being laughed at.

LilMissSunshine: I'm really sorry.

Nate31: Maybe I could open up to U if I knew ur real name. It's hard to think about talking to someone called Sunshine.

. . .

If you don't want to, never mind. I'm tired anyway. Speak another time.

LilMissSunshine: Don't go.

. . .

It's Alex, OK? I've got a boy's name.

Nate31: Not a boy's name. Short for Alexandra?

LilMissSunshine: Not short for anything. Mum's not into that. Some people call me Lexi. Whatever.

Nate31: It's pretty. Like you. Lovely Lexi

LilMissSunshine: Creepy.

Nate31: LOL. Joking.

LilMissSunshine: So will you talk to me now? What's the problem?

Nate31: It's kind of stupid but I need a girl's eye view. You are a real girl right? Not one of those internet robots you hear about.

LilMissSunshine: Ha ha.

Nate31: Here's the thing. There's this girl at school. She's kind of stalking me. We hooked up once, but we were both wasted. I'm not into her like that, but she won't take no, y'know? She keeps turning up at practice and just follows me around like a kicked puppy. What do I say to get her to leave it out? I don't want to make her do anything stupid.

LilMissSunshine: U've got a groupie!

Nate31: I guess. It isn't funny any more though. She knows where I live.

LilMissSunshine: Shouldn't have hooked up with a psycho.

Nate31: Is that all U got?

LilMissSunshine: Thinking.

Nate31: Wish I could talk to U face to face. Bet your boyfriend wouldn't like that, though.

LilMissSunshine: No BF here.

Nate31: Good

. . .

Shit. I mean

. . .

U know what I mean. Have U finished thinking?

LilMissSunshine: LOL. Still thinking. Have U said anything to make her think she had a chance?

Nate31: Maybe, at the party. Didn't think she'd take it seriously. Everyone drunk and hooking up. Am I a dickhead?

LilMissSunshine: Probably a bit ☺. U'll have to speak to her.

Nate31: What do I say? Maybe I could say I've met someone else and my girlfriend is the jealous type.

LilMissSunshine: Could work. And if U know someone else who might like her, you could point her in that direction.

Nate31: Like a consolation prize?

LilMissSunshine: NO. Make her feel wanted and special, even if it's not by U, big head.

Nate31: So if she asks about my girlfriend I could say I met her online?

LilMissSunshine: Whatever you like.

Nate31: I could say her name's Lexi.

. . .

LilMissSunshine: Like I said, say whatever you like!

Nate31: U'd get her off my back if I can say it's U. I printed out ur picture. It's in my wallet.

LilMissSunshine: SRSLY, y?

Nate31: I look at it when I'm feeling down, when I think about talking to U it makes me feel better. I even think about U when I'm playing hockey. It's doing my game no good. I just want to know everything about U. It's killing me.

LilMissSunshine: What is?

Nate31: I don't even know how far away U are from me. U could be hours away for all I know. Lands End, John o' Groats.

LilMissSunshine: LOL. Not that far away I bet.

Nate31: So where are U?

. . .

Lexi?

. . .

U could just tell me the county. No personal deets to upset ur mum!

. . .

Hey, it's OK if U don't want to tell me. No harm no foul. I'll still be thinking of U. Wishing you were nearby.

LilMissSunshine: OK. I guess that would be all right. I'm in Gloucestershire.

Nate31: NO WAY, me too.

LilMissSunshine: Way.

Nate31: Which town?

LilMissSunshine: Stroud.

Nate31: Can't believe this. I'm only the other side of Gloucester, about forty minutes from U. I can practically wave to U. Waving now.

LilMissSunshine: Waving back.

Nate31: U can't tell me this isn't meant to be. Out of everyone on the Internet, in the whole world, we meet each other online and live so close by.

LilMissSunshine: Maybe it is meant to be . . . maybe there is something to your theories after all. Crazy.

Nate31: Knew u'd come round.

LilMissSunshine: Gotta go, Mum wants a movie. Good luck with ur stalker. Let me know how it goes.

Nate31: Nite. I'll be dreaming of U.

LilMissSunshine: TTYL xx

You have a new text message

Alex: He says he lives close by. Think he's going to suggest a meet.

Ellie: Don't say ur going to go!

Alex: Haven't made any decisions. He hasn't suggested anything yet.

Ellie: But he will?

Alex: Definitely.

Face2Face

Nate31: U there?

LilMissSunshine: Hi. How'd it go?

Nate31: U were right. She ate it up about Cam and how he likes her and I can't step on his toes. U're so clever. Really glad I asked U what 2 do.

LilMissSunshine: Happy to help ☺ How was practice?

Nate31: Not bad. New boy on the team, cocked up a few of the passes, but I pulled off a few nice shots and a couple of goals. U don't really care about that.

LilMissSunshine: I care if U care.

Nate31: That's really cool of U. I imagined U were there watching. Helped my game!

LilMissSunshine: HTH. I'm being so useful today!

Nate31: LOL. So how was school at ur end? You changed out of ur uniform yet?

LilMissSunshine: Not yet. Can't be bothered.

Nate31: God, I always strip off first chance. Get that school vibe off me!

LilMissSunshine: Wanted to get online and see if U were home. I'll change L8R.

Nate31: ☺ Help me picture U while we talk. What's ur uniform like? Red like ur sports kit?

LilMissSunshine: Yeah, BRIGHT red. Major ick.

Nate31: Bet U go to one of those posh schools with a blazer!

LilMissSunshine: God no. We do have to wear kilts, though.

Nate31: ROFL. No way. Bet that looks amazing! The boys too?

LilMissSunshine: Not.

Nate31: Bet a man came up with that idea! Girls in kilts. School-girl fantasy material.

LilMissSunshine: Easy!

Nate31: Sorry.

LilMissSunshine: So what about urs – what's urs like?

Nate31: Dead simple actually – all black.

LilMissSunshine: Well jel

Nate31: U gotta send me a pic!

LilMissSunshine: God no.

Nate31: Go on. I so want to see ur gorgeous smile while we talk. It's strange speaking to the same photo all the time. Do a selfie!

LilMissSunshine: Oh all right.

Attachment

There U go. Don't laugh.

Nate31: If the girls in my school looked like that, more boys would stay on for A levels!

LilMissSunshine: Shut up!

Nate31: Stepbitch is shouting again. Gotta get out of the house. I'll poke U when I've found a place to hide out.

LilMissSunshine: Where U gonna go?

Nate31: Dunno, McDonalds maybe. Spk L8R.

Face2Face

To LilMissSunshine: Nate31 has poked you.

LilMissSunshine: RUOK?

Nate31: Yeah. No worries. She'll calm down in a couple of hours and I'll go back. Meanwhile I got fries, coke and wifi! LOL.

LilMissSunshine: Sounds like heaven.

Nate31: McD heaven! Every time she starts in on me, I think of U and it helps. U're my angel, U know that?

LilMissSunshine: Cos *heaven*. Clever.

Nate31: I'm serious, though.

. . .

Do U think about me?

LilMissSunshine: I do actually. Talking to U is the best bit of my day ATM.

Nate31: U having problems at school?

LilMissSunshine: Sort of. Sixth form – it's harder than I thought it would be!

Nate31: Tell me about it. So glad it's almost over n I can start working.

LilMissSunshine: Not going to uni?

Nate31: No way – seems stupid to go get into loads of debt when I can be earning hard cash. Stepbitch agreed not to nag me about uni so long as I got decent A levels. She keeps leaving brochures and shit around, but she can't say anything. I got a job lined up working for my uncle. Gotta wear a suit, but it'll be worth it. What about U, R U going to uni? Or art school, maybe?

LilMissSunshine: That would be amazing. Not sure I'm good enough, though.

Nate31: U R!

LilMissSunshine: Thanks ☺ Not sure my teachers think so.

Nate31: If they don't, they're crazy. And by the time u're a starving art student I'll be able to take U out properly. I can treat U when U run out of food and let U use my washing machine to do ur laundry! LOL.

LilMissSunshine: Sounds great.

Nate31: I mean it. I'll take U to any nice place U want.

LilMissSunshine: McDs heaven?

Nate31: If U like. But I'll be earning enough – we could go somewhere posh.

LilMissSunshine: With lots of forks?

Nate31: And three different types of wine glasses.

LilMissSunshine: I wouldn't fit in. LOL.

Nate31: U would. Maybe we should practise. I've got a bit of money saved. I could take U out somewhere. There's a really nice Chinese in Gloucester. . .

LilMissSunshine: U want to meet up???

Nate31: God, sorry, didn't mean to spring that on U. But yeah. I really want to meet U. Find out if u're as sweet in person!

. . .

Look, no pressure and definitely no rush. Maybe in a few weeks, when U know me better . . . just something to think about.

LilMissSunshine: Something to look forward to, you mean!

Nate31: ☺

Nate31: McDs is closing up. Hadn't realised it had got so late. Going to have to head home. Spk tmrw! xx

You have a new text message

Alex: He's mentioned meeting up. I'm going to do it.

Ellie: U can't.

Alex: It's the only way to be sure that he's the one.

Ellie: What if he's not what U think?

Alex: It'll be all right, El. Just don't tell anyone.

Ellie: I wouldn't. U know that. Just . . . be careful.

Face2Face

Nate31: Hi. R U there?

LilMissSunshine: How was ur day?

Nate31: My brother's getting on my nerves. Keeps breaking into my room.

LilMissSunshine: U should put a lock on the door.

Nate31: Stepbitch would love that!

LilMissSunshine: How old is he? Younger?

Nate31: Yeah. He's like 13 and all up in my grill. U got a brother?

LilMissSunshine: No. I'm an only child.

Nate31: U're so lucky.

LilMissSunshine: Not so sure about that.

Nate31: Does that mean u're spoiled rotten?

LilMissSunshine: WTH?

Nate31: Kidding. Just that's what they say about an only child isn't it?

LilMissSunshine: It's not all it's cracked up to be, believe me.

Nate31: No one hogging the TV remote. No one nicking ur stuff. No one eating all the breakfast cereal and drinking milk out of the bottle before U can use it. . .

LilMissSunshine: No one to lend you stuff. No one to laugh with while u're watching TV. No one to talk to. No one to tell secrets to. . .

Nate31: U've got ME now.

LilMissSunshine: Not like we can watch TV together.

Nate31: We could. What do U like watching?

LilMissSunshine: Not sports if that's what U mean.

Nate31: There must be something on now that U fancy? C'mon, switch on the TV. We can chat while we watch the same thing.

LilMissSunshine: There's nothing on.

Nate31: America's Next Top Model?

LilMissSunshine: SRSLY

Nate31: Bake Off?

LilMissSunshine: Dude, just because I'm a girl!

Nate31: I love Bake Off.

LilMissSunshine: Maybe we should do this another time. We could get the same movie on demand.

Nate31: What do U like?

LilMissSunshine: Kingsmen?

Nate31: Sounds good. U seen it B4?

LilMissSunshine: No. Like the sound of it, though.

Nate31: Me too. Movie night tmrw?

LilMissSunshine: OK.

Nate31: Ur mum will be OK with that?

LilMissSunshine: No worries. Parents R out every Thursday night.

Nate31: No sitter?

LilMissSunshine: Pur-lease!

Nate31: LOL. Just checkin.

LilMissSunshine: What about urs?

Nate31: Telly in my room. No problem. U gonna get popcorn and watch in your jammies?

LilMissSunshine: Is that how U watch a movie?

Nate31: Of course. We should have a virtual sleepover. U n me, in our jammies, up all night, chatting, watching movies and eating crap.

LilMissSunshine: Sounds great. Although school Friday.

Nate31: Well, if U don't want to. . .

LilMissSunshine: I want to.

Nate31: It's a date . . . well a pre-date.

LilMissSunshine: What's a pre-date?

Nate31: A date before the real date. U still want to meet up, right?

LilMissSunshine: I really do.

Nate31: We should make a real date – something to look forward to. Maybe a Thursday, then U don't have to worry ur mum.

LilMissSunshine: That sounds good. I'm busy next week, but how about in a fortnight?

Nate31: U're busy? What R U doing?

LilMissSunshine: Just BFF stuff.

Nate31: Thought I was ur BFF!

LilMissSunshine: RL BFF.

Nate31: I'm hurt ☹

LilMissSunshine: U'll live.

. . .

Nate?

Nate31: No really, I'm kind of hurt.

LilMissSunshine: I didn't mean to hurt ur feelings.

Nate31: Well, how about U meet me after?

LilMissSunshine: Could be L8. The restaurant will be shut.

Nate31: I can get takeaway – bring it to somewhere nr U.

LilMissSunshine: Like where?

Nate31: How about Stratford Park?

LilMissSunshine: Won't it be cold?

Nate31: U could bundle up. It'll be romantic. I'll wait for U under the trees by the pond. How about midnight?

LilMissSunshine: I guess that would work.

Nate31: Don't sound too enthusiastic. I'm excited about meeting U IRL, but if U don't want to. . .

LilMissSunshine: I want to. Really. I'll be there.

Nate31: Promise?

LilMissSunshine: Promise.

Nate31: It's going to be an incredible night. I love U, Lexi.

. . .

It's OK, U don't have to say it back. Movie night tmrw.

LilMissSunshine: Can't wait.

. . .

Love U too.

You have a new text message

Alex: He says he loves me.

Ellie: U're meeting him then?

Alex: In Stratford Park.

Ellie: When?

Alex: Thursday. Midnight. I've got some prep to do.

Ellie: PLEASE be careful.

Alex: U know me.

Ellie: That's what I'm worried about.

Alex: Just make sure U do ur part. U've got the name?

Ellie: Carl Matthews, right?

Alex: Just don't fall asleep or anything.

Ellie: U can trust me. I just wish U wouldn't meet him.

Police Report
Case No: 16546789
Date: 9/10/2015
Reporting Officer: DC Carl Matthews
Prepared by: DS Jackson
Detail of event:

On 9/10/2015 at 12.15 a.m. personnel from Gloucestershire Constabulary and paramedics from Gloucestershire Royal Hospital, responded to an emergency call in the Stratford Park area, logged at 12.03 a.m. (a transcript of the call appears as Appendix A to this document).

The witness, who refused to give her name, asked to speak to DC Carl Matthews directly and claimed that there was a teenage girl in trouble at the central pond in Stratford Park.

On attending the scene, DC Matthews discovered teenager Alex Trelawney (see Appendix B), along with a middle-aged man whom she claimed had groomed her online and was now attempting to seduce her.

The man, upon seeing the officers, attempted to flee and had to be restrained and cuffed. Miss Trelawney appeared to be expecting the officers, DC Matthews in particular and, while the man denied her allegations, she handed over printouts of their correspondence wherein he clearly portrays himself as a teenage boy named Nate.

Although the man refused to identify himself at the scene, a car was found parked by the south exit of the park which contained his fingerprints. DVLA records subsequently gave us the name of Michael Hanson (Appendix C).

Of particular concern to DC Matthews, the car boot appeared to have air holes cut into it and contained cable ties and plastic sheeting (photographed as evidence in Appendix D).

Miss Trelawney has willingly handed herself into the Barton Police Station, along with her evidence of the man's activities. The full transcript of her interview can be found in Appendix E.

The park has been closed while forensic evidence is gathered.

Initial findings are that Miss Alex Trelawney (aged 17) planned and executed a 'sting' in order to entrap the man she believes responsible for the disappearance in October 2014 of Livi Trelawney (aged 16), an incident also investigated by DC Matthews. Officers have warned Miss Trelawney against repeating her dangerous behaviour and her legal guardians (Mr Dean Trelawney and Mrs Angela Trelawney, recently divorced) have been informed.

You have a new text message

Ellie: What happened? Did the police turn up? Was it him?

Alex: Yeah. It was him.

Ellie: What would U have done if Nate had been some innocent teenager?

Alex: Started again. But I told U he was the one.

Ellie: U're sure he was the one who took Livi? Not some other pervert.

Alex: Definitely him.

Ellie: How do U know? Did he confess or something?

Alex: Because he took the bait. He wanted *ME*.

Ellie: What do U mean?

Alex: A year after her murder, he had to be looking for another girl. How could he resist someone so like her?

Ellie: U lied to him.

Alex: Just enough.

Ellie: You played 'Livi'.

Alex: I played 'Lexi'.

Ellie: And how do U feel now? Better?

Alex: Not really. Still empty – she's still gone.

Ellie: I love U, U know that don't U?

Alex: I love U too.

Face2Face

Hello, friend. You haven't checked your profile in a while. Why not see if anyone wants to chat with you. . .?

One year earlier. . .

You have a new text message

Livi: U still awake?

Livi: Need to talk to U.

Livi: Wake up.

Alex: WTH? It's 3am. U bin on Chatz all nite?

Livi: I'm in love. Really in love.

Alex: Go 2 sleep. Tlk TMRW.

Livi: He's my soulmate, Alex. He's perfect. He plays county hockey, so I know he's ripped. He's got girls all over him – even has his own stalker, LOL! He's doing A levels, so he's only a little bit older and his stepmum lets him do whatever he wants. He can meet me any time. He's going to take me out to dinner somewhere really posh. He says I'm totally special. I've made up my mind. I'm going to meet him.

Alex: When?

Livi: Now.

Alex: OMG. We need to talk about this properly. Don't do anything stupid.

Livi: Not stupid. Me n Curt R meant to be 2gether. Climbing out of window right now.

Alex: OMG, OMG. Don't you dare!

Livi: Already gone.

Alex: Mum'll go spare.

Livi: Don't care.

Alex: Wait till Fri. I'll come with you after netball.

Livi: Don't need U. I'll be fine. We don't have to do everything 2gether, just because we're twins. This is MY boyfriend.

Alex: At least tell me where u're going!

Alex: Livi?

Alex: Where?

Livi: Don't tell.

Alex: WHERE?

Livi: Stratford Park. Moonlight picnic. Romantic.

Alex: Suspicious.

Livi: Don't be a downer!!!

Alex: Sorry. ☹ Be careful. Text me when u're back. Tell me all about it.

Alex: Livi R U back yet?

Alex: Cldn't sleep. Been up for hours. Worried now. Just text me.

Alex: Almost time for school.

Alex: Livi. Please. ☹

Alex: Livi ☹☹☹

A LEVEL PLAYING FIELD

by Paula Rawsthorne

Adrenaline surges around my body as the announcement comes over the speakers. 'The final of the men's 200 metres individual medley.'

I'm desperate to get out there, like a twitching horse in the starting gates, but I have to wait as three other guys are announced before me. Then it's my turn.

'In lane five, representing Great Britain, Alfie Pickford!'

I stride out of the tunnel onto poolside. There's a glare of lights and a wall of noise as thousands of spectators in the Amsterdam stadium whistle and whoop. I raise my arms to greet them.

All the other swimmers have headphones on, pumping music getting them into the zone, but I don't need it. I want to be in the moment. I need to hear the crowd, feel the electricity crackling around the pool. I soak up the smell of the chlorine, the lights shimmering off the surface of the water, the echoing claps in the air – that's my soundtrack. I feed off it like a rock star feeds off the energy of his audience.

I take a sideways glance at the Canadian in lane four. He's my main competition. He was the fastest in the heats and has been posting impressive times all year. Sure, he's got a couple of inches on me, but I'm leaner and packing more muscle. I've been studying his form with

Duncan, analysing videos of his races. 'Know your enemy,' Duncan always says. The Canadian is a fast finisher, but so am I now. I may be the youngest in this line-up but over the past three months my form has been building and today, right now, I'm in peak condition and ready to blow the rest of them out of the water.

My eyes search for Duncan. He's sitting by the other coaches. He looks calm and confident as he nods to me. Gary is with Mum and Dad in the stands. I can tell that he's overheated in his expensive suit and tie. He knows how hot it gets in the aquatic stadiums but he always insists that an agent should look 'the business', especially when the TV cameras are rolling. Mum blows me a kiss and holds up crossed fingers. Dad waves a Union Jack, his face in a rictus smile of stress. There's no Lily, of course – the world championships, the biggest race of my life, no wonder she isn't here.

Mum and Dad tried their best to persuade her. They even said that they'd pay for her to go to Glastonbury if she just came along and looked like she actually supported her twin brother. Gary is keen for her to be more visible. He's seen photos of Lily, thinks she's beautiful, says the public will really go for the 'twin thing'. He reckons we're a photogenic family and he loves the fact that Dad is a taxi driver – says we're the kind of 'northern salt of the earth people' the public likes to get behind. Gary's from London – he says patronising stuff like that, but I don't mind because he's great at his job.

Anyway, it's best Lily isn't here. She'd probably be scowling at me, sending out bad vibes. I reckon me and Lily would have been close. Before we went to school Mum says we were inseparable. She'd take us to playgroups but we weren't interested in mixing with any other kids when we had each other. When we started school they put us in different classes. The head told Mum that, in her experience, it helped twins to establish their own identity and friendship group. Mum was fine but me and Lily weren't having any of it. We were miserable without each other and couldn't wait for playtime to be together. But then things changed – the swimming got in the way.

I was only five when Robbie spotted me in the local pool. He said that I was darting around as fast as a guppy chasing food in a fish tank. Straight away he knew I had potential. He asked my mum and dad if I'd like to join the swimming club. 'Your lad has practically got gills,' he said to them. Lily was still doing widths by the time I was doing my bronze. She wasn't interested and, after a while, she gave up swimming all together. For the first few years my swimming didn't really affect her apart from her being dragged along to watch the lessons. She mostly sat poolside doing homework, but then I started swimming for the club and then the county and that meant more evenings and weekends were taken up by training and meets.

I know that Mum felt bad. She made sure that she enrolled Lily in dance lessons to make up for it but Mum was never able to take her. Instead, she was always asking other parents to transport her and Lily just got embarrassed. There was a time when Lily was proud of me, but over the years that pride has turned into resentment. I can remember the actual day it all became too much for her.

We were eleven and Mum and Dad were standing in the kitchen arguing in front of us about who had to go to her dance show and who got to go to my meet in Newcastle. I remember the look of hurt on her face as she shouted at them, 'I don't want either of you there. I know that you don't want to come. You'd rather be at Alfie's competition, so just go!'

Mum had tried to hug her but she'd pushed her away. 'I'm sorry, Lily, it's not that we don't want to be at your show, it's just that we all have to make sacrifices. Of course the show is important but, at the end of the day, your dance is just a hobby. Swimming is Alfie's life, his chance of a career. Robbie says he has the talent to go all the way. If we didn't back him one hundred per cent we'd never forgive ourselves.'

As soon as Mum and Dad decided that Lily was old enough to be left on her own she stopped coming to the meets and, by the time we were thirteen, Lily had got in with a group of older kids who were known for being trouble. She started staying out late, messing around in school, going out with boys.

I tried to talk to her, apologise for all the time Mum and Dad spent with me, but she said that she didn't care, that I'd done her a favour because they were too busy to hassle her. She said that she felt sorry for me, that I had no life and no fun, that Mum and Dad didn't expect anything of her – all the pressure was on their 'Golden Boy'.

I can see the rest of the GB squad clustered down one end of the stands, holding up a big poster of Nemo with my face stuck on it. I try to block them out – now isn't the time to get irritated. Gary won't be happy. He's told me that the nickname is too childish for a seventeen-year-old. He says that we need a 'rebrand', a name that conveys the right image for an elite athlete.

I've been known as Nemo for years. It started at school. Girls called me it because they thought it was cute, but the boys picked up on it to make me look stupid, put me down. They've always been jealous – jealous that girls fancy me, jealous that I get time off school for meets, jealous that I'm good at what I do, better than good. At school some lads think they can take the piss, but in the pool they wouldn't mess with me. I'm a shark cruising through the water, striking fear into everything around me.

I unzip my tracksuit top and slip out of the bottoms. I place them into the plastic box behind my block and begin my warm up ritual. I bend down and scoop water from the pool to splash on my face and chest like I'm anointing myself. I lower the goggles from my cap and position them. I like to feel the suction and tightness around my eyes sockets. I'm sealed in, focused, impenetrable.

I windmill my shoulders, stretching my arms, rolling my head, and then I step up onto the block. The pool is so still and calm, no trace of the last race that churned it up like a shipping lane.

Silence descends on the stadium. It's as if everyone is holding their breath.

'On your marks.' I curl my fingers around the edge of the block, legs bent, body arched, every fibre poised, all senses heightened like a cheetah waiting to pounce on its prey. I lean forward just a fraction.

BEEP!

I dive from the block, slicing just under the water and pushing forward with powerful dolphin kicks. I'm already metres along the pool by the time I break the surface and take a breath, powering along with my butterfly stroke. I'm dragging the water with my shovel-like hands and propelling my streamlined body with flipper-sized feet.

Being in water feels as natural to me as standing on dry land. Before all the pressure of competition built up, I used to love the freedom of swimming. It was like entering a different world where I could clear my head of all of life's crap. It was just me, cutting through the water, focusing on my stroke, on my breathing, gliding up and down the pool almost in a trance.

Robbie stuck with me for years. He coached me up the ranks, never missed a training session, travelled to every meet to support me. He was there to see me through the disappointments as well as the wins. I know that he sacrificed a lot for me. Jacqui, his wife, used to say, 'You see more of him than I do!' She'd laugh, but she wasn't joking.

I wanted to do well for Robbie but sometimes the weight of his expectations made my head pound. It's the same with Mum and Dad. They've spent a fortune that they haven't got so that I can 'fulfil my potential'. No matter how many times Mum says, 'Just do your best', I know that they want to see me go all the way. I know that they dream of me standing on the podium at the Olympics with a gold medal around my neck. Anything less and I'll feel like I've let them down.

My fingertips touch the wall and I turn onto my back in one fluid movement. It's too close to gauge who's in front – there are only fractions of seconds in it. I just have to concentrate on my backstroke, my head tilted out of the water, my arms powering past my ears, my muscular legs pummelling the water.

Even when I'm asleep the swimming doesn't stop. I've always had dreams about being in the water but recently they've changed into nightmares. Over the last few weeks one keeps recurring – I'm way ahead in a race, feeling unstoppable, but all of a sudden I'm being dragged down to the bottom of the pool. I flail around, panicking, realising that there are weights chained to my ankles. As I look up I can see the shimmering bodies of the other swimmers powering above me but no one notices that I've gone under . . . that I'm drowning. I wake up gasping for breath, sweat pouring off me.

I've kept the nightmare to myself. It's best not to give Mum and Dad anything else to stress about.

I felt really bad when we dumped Robbie, but we would have been mad not to go with Duncan. He's a world-class coach and he came looking for me! Duncan said that Robbie is a nice bloke but that he's an amateur and that I'd outgrown him. Mum and Dad agreed – it was time to move on. I needed a pro like Duncan to take me to the next level, and he's done that and more. With Robbie it was like I was stuck at Everest's base camp, but after eight months with Duncan I'm within touching distance of the summit. There's no way that I'd have got to the final of the world championships if I'd stayed with Robbie. No way!

Duncan knows his stuff. Straight away he put me on a hard-core training programme. The gym work has built my muscle mass and the aerobic exercise has increased my lung capacity and stamina. And he's got me eating properly. No more double burger and chips after a session. He says to think of my body as a machine that needs daily maintenance to keep it in peak condition. Sure, it's boring and I spend an unhealthy amount of time thinking about curries and Chinese takeaways, but it's worth it. You don't get to the top without self-discipline and sacrifice.

And Duncan treats me like a man, not a kid. If I've messed up a race, made some stupid mistake on the turn or been too slow off the blocks, then he gives me a bollocking. He's not like, 'Don't worry about it, son. You'll do better next time.' He's more like, 'What the f—k was that? If you haven't got what it takes then there are plenty of swimmers as good as you that I can go and coach.' It stresses me out, but it works. I train harder for longer. I push my body until I can hardly drag myself out of the pool.

But Duncan has taught me that it's not just the physical side of it. Half the battle is mental. He taps my forehead hard and says, 'To be a winner you have to behave like a winner, think like a winner!'

He has me doing this 'visualisation' technique. I have to imagine every second of swimming my perfect race. I can see my body rocketing through the water like a torpedo, leaving the competition behind. I can see my fingertips touching the wall first. I conjure up the feeling of euphoria as I realise that I've won!

'Do you like that feeling?' Duncan asks.

'Sure, it's the best feeling in the world,' I reply.

'Well, only winning produces it. Coming second just feels like failure,' Duncan says.

When I was with Robbie he wasn't keen on me getting an agent. He reckoned that agents just distract athletes with money-making schemes so they can take their cut. He said that I had to concentrate one hundred per cent on the swimming. That's one of the differences between Robbie and Duncan – Duncan has vision. Duncan says that being an elite swimmer opens up doors, if you know where to knock. He says that we have to look to the future.

It was Duncan who introduced me to Gary. Gary took us to this really posh restaurant in London where loads of celebrities go. I spotted

Dwayne Johnson in the corner behind the fish tank. I was desperate to go and ask for his autograph but Gary said that it wouldn't be cool to disturb him. So I just walked past him when I went to the loo and took a photo on my phone. He pretended not to notice.

The food at the restaurant was pretty crap. The portions were tiny and they didn't even have chips on the menu but it was great just being there. The stories Gary told me! The guy knows everyone, even people who aren't his clients. He told me about this pool party at the Beckhams' house in LA. He's not a bullshitter. He showed me the photos on his phone. Him with his arm around Becks – unreal!

Gary was giving it loads. 'Alfie, you're a good-looking lad. You're very marketable. I can see some modelling and TV work. You're the type who appeals to the mums and daughters. Good looking in an . . . unthreatening way. There are a couple of things we'd have to work on. You could do with a few sessions on the sunbed and we could get your teeth whitened.'

'What's wrong with my teeth?' I asked.

'Nothing, but it's all about the dazzling Hollywood smile these days.' He winked.

At the end of the dinner Gary gave me a gift-wrapped box.

He said, 'Whether you decide to go with me or not I want you to have this as a sign of how much I admire your talent, but don't open it here. Wait till you get home.'

As soon as me and Duncan were on the train I ripped it open. I actually screamed when I saw it. It was a Rolex – no joke, a genuine freakin' Rolex. I looked it up. It's worth over four grand. I phoned him from the train sounding like a right idiot, all over-excited and not able to put a sentence together.

Gary was laughing. 'You sign with me and one day you'll get paid for wearing a Rolex.'

Before I signed the contract with Gary he gave me a big lecture. He said, 'I'll get you a deal with the biggest water-sports sponsors on the planet, but they're looking for ambassadors for their brand, so they don't want to see photos of you falling over drunk or snorting coke in the toilets of some club – and don't be going with any groupies. Before you know it they will have sold their story to some red top and you'll look like a sleaze – the mums won't like it.'

I rolled my eyes. *Groupies, nightclubs! I wish!*

There have been girls I fancy and I know a few of them fancy me, but I've never had time for them. Anyway, who'd want to go out with me? Up at 5.30 to get to the pool. An hour's training before grabbing breakfast on my way to school. Straight back to the pool after lessons, then into the gym for weights and circuit training. I spend the rest of the evening eating all this tasteless food Duncan has got me on and trying to get my homework done. Then, before I crash into bed completely knackered, I take another shower to try to scrub the chlorine off me, but I don't think I'll ever do it – it's ingrained in my skin. No matter how much aftershave I splash on, there's always a whiff of bleached toilets about me.

I've paced it well, my rhythm is smooth, a hundred metres down and I'm feeling good. I touch the wall and turn, kicking off with my feet, gliding under the water until I break the surface and fill my lungs with the warm air. I breaststroke down lane five like a supersonic frog. But as my head bobs in and out of the water I can feel a burn building in my lungs. Out the corner of my eye I see the Canadian edging ahead of me. I can't let him! I won't let him! I've worked too hard for this, put everything on the line.

I've been letting things get to me recently and it's not good because I need to stay focused. Last week Mum was hauled into school. They said that I was rude to a dinner lady, which I was, but she deserved it. I always have the chicken salad on a Tuesday – I need the protein – but when I got to the front of the queue she'd given the last portion away.

'Sorry, son.' She smiled. 'It's been popular today.'

The next second I was leaning over the counter shouting at her, 'Why didn't you save me any? You know that I have that on a Tuesday, you stupid cow!'

Her face turned to thunder and she roared at me. 'Don't you talk to me like that!'

And other things have been getting to me, like the zits that have appeared all over my face. Mum thinks it's the stress of the big competition. I know what's caused them but I can't tell her. These zits are red and angry – it's like all the aggression I'm trying to keep inside is erupting out of my skin.

Gary wasn't pleased when he saw me. He told me that if I win today the *Mail* will do a feature. He said, 'We'll have to slap a bit of foundation on you and if that doesn't work they can always airbrush the photos.'

He's been bigging me up to the media and filling them in about the sacrifices that my parents have made for me – Dad doing all those extra shifts, Mum getting up at the crack of dawn to ferry me to training before going to work as a carer. Gary's suggested that they get a photo of me and Mum surrounded by the old people at the nursing home. He said the *Mail* loved the idea.

The Canadian's turned before me! He's a whole body length ahead, leaving me in his wake. It's the last length. I am not going to let this bastard beat me! Crawl is my strongest stroke. I've just got to concentrate, ignore the muscle spasms, ignore the burning, stay focused.

Last month we got home from a big meet really late and found kids spilling out of our front door, sprawled in the driveway, throwing up on the pavement. I didn't recognise most of them. The music was throbbing all down the street. The neighbours were out in their dressing gowns. They gave Mum a right earful.

The house was trashed, sofas upturned, carpets soaked in booze, the TV was hanging off the wall. Two lads were laying into each other in the kitchen. Some girl was dancing on the table with all my medals around her neck! I grabbed them off her and ran upstairs looking for Lily. I found her half naked with some bloke in Mum and Dad's bed, an empty bottle of vodka on the floor. I bawled at her and she just gave me the finger, saying, 'Piss off, Nemo.'

I heard a siren outside. That's when I lost it. I grabbed her arm and dragged her off the bed. I lifted her off her feet and slammed her against the wall. 'You bitch! Do you want this to get in the papers? Two weeks before the biggest competition of my life! Is this what all this is about, trying to ruin my career because you're a talentless, jealous slag?'

Her glazed eyes widened, her lipstick-smeared mouth gaped open in shock.

I gasped. My hands shot open and she slid down the wall. Red angry handprints marked her arms.

She found her voice. 'You prick. I hate you!'

Twenty metres to go but I'm closing the gap. I'm in line with his feet, his torso, his shoulders. We're neck and neck but I can sense him slowing. He's got nothing else to give as I surge ahead with a last burst of energy and my fingertips stretch for the wall. I hear the roar of the crowd as I turn and look up at the board displaying my name as the winner. I can't take it in. I've smashed my personal best. I've set a new world record. I pant and pump the air – no breath left to speak.

The Canadian slaps my back but his face is granite. 'That was unreal, man. I've never seen anyone finish that fast.'

Is that a compliment or an accusation? I give him a million-dollar smile. I won't let paranoia ruin my moment.

I haul myself out of the pool and soak in the adulation of the crowd. I throw my goggles and cap up into the stands to cheers and whoops. Mum and Dad are jumping and shouting, 'We love you Alfie. We're so proud of you!' Gary's already on his phone making deals. Most of the GB squad look ecstatic, though a couple of them are just clapping politely – jealous gits.

Duncan rushes towards me, cupping my wet face with his hands.

'What did I tell you, Alfie? Stick with me and I'll take you all the way. Olympics, here we come!' He beams.

It was about three months ago that Duncan had his 'chat' with me. I'd just come fourth in the two hundred metres medley at the British Championships. I'd been overdoing it and my body was protesting; that race felt like I was wading through a swamp. I knew that I wouldn't qualify for the Olympic team if I couldn't find my form. Duncan invited me round to his flat. He sat me down and told me that I was at a make-or-break point in my career. He said I wasn't going to be able to win unless I was prepared to make an uncomfortable decision.

I asked him what he meant and he sighed. 'Most of the swimmers you're competing against are doping, but you know that, don't you?'

I felt my stomach lurch. Of course there'd always been rumours flying around but I'd never seen any evidence of it.

'How can you be sure?' I asked.

He gave me an unflinching stare. 'When you've been around as long as I have, you get to know these things. There are some really big names that you'd be shocked about.'

'So you're saying I should dope, that I should cheat?'

'Alfie, it isn't cheating if everyone is doing it. All you'd be doing is making a level playing field for yourself.'

I couldn't believe what he was saying. I was outraged. I told him to get lost. I stormed out of his flat and went home, but I didn't say anything to Mum and Dad. I couldn't sleep all that night and the next morning I phoned him. In the end I was too easy to persuade. I knew that I couldn't win clean against dopers and if I couldn't win I'd have wasted my entire life. I'd be dropped by Duncan, dropped by Gary. I was seventeen and I had no life outside the pool, no proper mates, no other interests. I was even having to resit because I'd messed up my exams with all the training. And how could I face Mum and Dad after everything they'd done for me? If I didn't dope I'd fail and be left with nothing. I didn't have any other choice.

Duncan guaranteed that I'd be in safe hands. He said that he was putting himself on the line just as much as I was. He said that he knew the very best people. There's a lab he uses, a doctor, an undetectable new steroid specially developed to build up muscle mass and beat any drugs test. He said that it can't be detected in urine or blood; that, right now, he knew three swimmers using it and they'd passed test after test. 'You just have to get the timing right,' he said.

I was still feeling sick about it. Every athlete knows how sophisticated the anti-doping testing is getting – always trying to unmask the latest performance-enhancing substance. The more dopers they uncover, the harder they're coming down on them. If I got caught I'd be banned for God knows how long but, worse than that, once you've been found doping your reputation is destroyed. Even if I stayed clean for the rest of my career there'd always be doubt, resentment from other athletes. No matter how many medals I won clean I'd never be seen as a national hero and no sponsor would touch me.

But Duncan told me to trust him and to never tell a soul.

'I don't care if it's the press, a FINA official or your parents, if you're ever asked if you're doping, deny it, deny it, deny it! Be disgusted at the very suggestion.'

Over the last three months I've had a few steroid injections in preparation for big meets. I nearly wet myself when I was randomly tested five weeks ago, but Duncan was right, the results came back clean, not a trace. The steroids make me feel invincible, powerful, but they're not without their downside.

I'd read all about the side effects but when I asked Duncan he said not to worry. He said that doctors and FINA just exaggerate to scare people off. He reckons most people don't experience any. But I have – the zits, the aggression – I've been really struggling to hold it together.

The Dutch official hovers with his clipboard as I do a poolside interview for the BBC. I smile into the camera and thank everyone – my coach, my parents, Team GB – I couldn't have done it without all their support and, yes, of course I'm ecstatic about the prospect of representing my country in the Olympics.

As soon as the interview ends the official ushers me away.

'Congratulations, Mr Pickford. Please come this way to the control station,' he says politely.

I'm cool about it. It's just routine. All winners get tested.

As I walk along, the spectators call out for a photo and autographs.

'Can I just do a few?' I ask him.

'I'm sorry.' He smiles tightly. 'Let's get the samples done first.'

I shout out to the crowd, laughing, 'Wait till the medal ceremony. I'll pose for all the selfies you want then!'

Before I disappear down the corridor to doping control, I turn around and soak in the scene in the stadium. I want this moment to last forever.

We fly home from Amsterdam the next day. I'm lying on my bed, knackered but still buzzing. Lily puts her head around my bedroom door. She isn't smiling but she says, 'I'm going out but I just wanted to say well done. I know how hard you've worked for this and I'm pleased for you.' She doesn't wait for a response. She disappears, leaving me grinning from ear to ear.

A phone rings downstairs. I don't pay any attention until I hear Mum's voice rising.

'His phone's off. He's resting. . . Well, why can't you just tell me? . . . What? . . . Well, obviously there's been a mistake at your end. . . Yes, I'll get him if it'll help clear up this ridiculous situation.'

'Alfie, love,' Mum shouts. 'Can you come down here a minute? A woman from the Anti- Doping Agency wants to talk to you, but I'm sure you can sort this out.'

I feel my stomach heave. I lean over the bed, spewing puke onto the carpet.

MAGPIE SOUP

by Dave Cousins

'Dad?' I knock on the bedroom door. 'Dad? It's me, Mina.'

The wood feels cold and slightly clammy when I press my ear against it. I listen to the silence on the other side for another few seconds, then turn the handle.

Dad is sitting on the side of the bed. He's wearing the white shirt I ironed late last night and the black tie we bought to go with his suit, but that's as far as he's got. Then I notice his boxer shorts, a present from me last Christmas – the ones with Homer Simpson's face all over them – do you remember? You said he'd never wear them.

'Mrs Radcliffe's here,' I tell him.

Dad's staring at something in his hands – a narrow gold band clamped between shaking fingers.

Just when I begin to think he hasn't heard me, he looks up. His eyes are red, and the salt and pepper stubble across his cheeks glistens with tears.

'The undertaker's here, Dad. We need to go soon.'

He stares at me for a moment, as though he isn't sure who I am, then he nods and stands up.

I stop him at the door. 'You should probably put some trousers on first.'

Again the look of confusion as he glances down at his bare legs, then turns back into the room.

'I'll tell her you're on your way,' I say, closing the door.

Mrs Radcliffe reminds me of that statue outside the library – the same look of granite-faced, gothic disapproval – except Mrs Radcliffe hasn't got pigeon shit highlights in her hair. If she had it might stop me staring at the huge monobrow sitting above her eyes like some kind of face pet. As I walk back into the front room I can hear your voice in my head – *You keep her talking, while I grab the tweezers and sort that thing out!*

The laugh is so unexpected I catch it late and announce my arrival in the room with a noise like a pig snort. Everybody looks at me and I feel my cheeks glow.

'He'll be out in a minute,' I say, staring them all down.

This is your house, Mina. Don't get pushed around on your own turf, girl! Too right.

'Would anybody like a drink?'

There's a collective murmur and raising of mugs, and I remember Celia has been shoving cups of tea and coffee into people's hands the moment they crossed the threshold. Mrs Radcliffe is holding your HOT STUFF! mug – the one where the bloke's clothes slowly disappear as the liquid inside cools down. Knowing Celia, she gave it to her on purpose. The undertaker doesn't seem to have noticed that she's holding a mug with a semi-naked man on it.

'How is your father this morning?' Mrs Radcliffe leans towards me and I catch a waft of strawberries. I had her down as more of a Chanel No 5 woman, but maybe she's all floaty pastel dresses and fruity soaps in her time off from being Bride of Dracula. *We all have our secrets.*

Do you remember that game we used to play? All those hours stuck in hospital waiting rooms surrounded by strangers – we'd go round making up names and occupations for everyone, coming up with whole backstories like we were creating characters for a book. The best part was always deciding what people's secrets were.

We all have secrets, Mina.

That's what you told me.

Of course I wanted to know what yours was.

If I told you, it wouldn't be a secret, would it?

It's not a secret now, though, is it, Mum? You were dying and now you're dead. Your secret's out.

We never made up horrible secrets like that for people, though. Most of ours were funny. Like the bored hospital porter we saw struggling to push trolleys bulging with dirty sheets into the lift. We gave him a complete double life: by day, mild-mannered hospital worker; by night, Gloria – glamorous drag queen and huge star on the Soho club circuit!

We used to see him a lot. Do you remember that time? When we were taking the lift down to the café and we saw him running to get in before the doors closed. You said – actually *said* out loud – *Hold the door for Gloria.* He heard you too. He was giving us funny looks all the way down and we couldn't stop giggling.

Shit!

Why did I have to think of that? Now my throat's gone all tight and dry and I can feel the heat behind my eyes – a warning that tears are on their way.

Not today. This is a celebration. That's what you wanted, right?

I want a party, Mina. A proper knees-up. I want people dancing, laughing, getting drunk and being sick in the garden. I want people to have something to remember me by.

So that's what we're doing. Unofficially. Celia's been brilliant, of course. I couldn't have done it without her. I don't know if I'd have had the nerve to go behind Dad's back if she hadn't been there reminding me that this is what you wanted – that we owed it to you.

We did try talking to Dad, but he was either off in another world or just refused to talk about it. Which isn't like him at all. One night he just exploded – started shouting at me to *leave it alone*, that he was *taking care of it*, that you were *his* wife and it was nothing to do with me.

Of course I shouted back that you were *my* mother, except the words stuck in my throat and I started crying, which really pissed me off. I mean, why do I have to start crying right in the middle of an argument when I'm trying to stand up to someone? It really ruins the effect.

It was all rubbish anyway. When Dad said he was taking care of it, what he meant was, he'd asked Mrs Radcliffe – the Princess of the Night – to take care of it for him.

Sod her! She never knew your mum – that's what Celia said. Which is when we decided to make our own . . . alternative arrangements.

So, this is for you, Mum.

All the surprises. For you.

I need to keep remembering that. It helps to stop my knees shaking so much. That's not just an expression either, they really are shaking. A few centimetres below the hem of my black school skirt my knees are knocking like something from a *Scooby-Doo* cartoon.

I just hope Dad forgives me.

Eventually.

When he calms down, he might understand I did it for you – that this is what you wanted.

I just wish you could have written it down somewhere so I could show him, prove it's not just something I conjured up for my own entertainment.

You know me, I get carried away sometimes, get caught up in the idea. I can see it all playing out like a movie and it's brilliant. Except when it's really happening, it's nothing like I imagined. It's a cold, damp Yorkshire day and the house is full of serious people in dark clothes, and Dad is so numb with grief that he's forgotten to put his trousers on. Now it doesn't feel like such a good idea – it feels like a disaster waiting to happen.

But it's too late to stop it. Everything has been arranged.

I just wish you were here. It would be OK if you were here with me. Though I don't suppose we'd be doing any of this if you were.

You said that at the hospital, remember? When you were scared. *It'll be OK if you're with me.* Well, it's payback time, Mum. If ever I needed you with me – now is the time.

Dad still hasn't come out of the bedroom and we can't leave without him. Part of me wants him to stay in there forever, so my plan will never be triggered into action. At the same time, I want to get it over with, because the waiting is killing me.

Sorry . . . bad choice of words.

Death hijacks everything. Things you say without thinking suddenly mean something else. Or you forget for a moment and find yourself laughing at the TV, then remember again and feel guilty. I know people are avoiding me today as much as I'm avoiding them. They're scared of me and Dad – scared of our grief. They don't know what to say, because nothing you say makes any difference. It's just words. But words are better than silence.

How can a room be packed full of people and still feel so empty? It's like everyone is holding their breath. It makes me want to pull a really loud armpit fart, or burp or something – anything to break the silence.

As I haven't got a burp brewing, and I don't think even I've got the nerve to do an armpit fart right now, I pull out my phone and plug it into Dad's stereo. By the way everyone in the room jumps when the song starts and then stares at me, I'm guessing you're not supposed to play music on the morning of a funeral. Tough! I need you here, Mum, and now you are.

Your favourite song fills the room, pushing back the shadows, breathing life into the stale, dead air. OK, the fact that the song is called 'Fortunately Gone' has never registered before. In the current circumstances it strikes me as somewhat ironic. I'm suddenly fighting back the urge to burst out laughing again because you would have loved that. You would have thrown your head back and laughed that loud, dirty laugh of yours and not cared what anyone thought.

How many times have I heard this song? Hundreds? Thousands? I know all the words off by heart though I don't remember ever learning them. They've just been there all my life – me and you singing along about magpie soup. That was the line I loved when I was little. I wanted to know what magpie soup would taste like – if there were real magpies in it.

You told me that magpies fill their nests with shiny things they like the look of, and that magpie soup was the same: a combination of all the things you liked, so it was different for each person who made it. You said it didn't matter if the ingredients didn't really go together – because how could it taste bad if it was made up of all my favourite things? I have to say, you set yourself up for disaster with that one, Mum. What was it we put in? Chocolate spread, mint ice cream, tomato soup and a banana! And you ate the lot! Said it was the most delicious magpie soup you'd ever tasted. . .

OK . . . not such a good idea to think about that right now.

'Your father is very lucky to have you, Mina.'

I realise Mrs Radcliffe is standing next to me, her pale eyes peering out from under the eyebrow creature.

She's not wrong, though.

Right up until you died, Dad was brilliant. Everyone said it was amazing how strong he was. But the moment you were gone, it was like his elastic broke.

The first sign was the smoking. I'd never seen him even hold a cigarette before. You remember how he always said you need strong lungs to get a noise out of a trombone? Then he stopped playing in the band altogether.

Celia didn't understand how significant that was, but then she didn't grow up round here. She couldn't believe I'd started playing trumpet when I was five. I told her how members of Dad's family have played in the Thackett Mill Brass Band for over a hundred years. I tried to explain how the band is like our extended family, a part of who we are – like different coloured threads in a carpet.

So when Dad stopped going, it meant something – it was a sign. Not that I really needed one. I could see what was happening right in front of my eyes. Dad acted like a zombie – confused all the time – like he wasn't really here any more. I don't think he would have eaten, or washed or anything if I hadn't been around to make him. To be honest it helped me having something to do – someone else to think about.

I'm about to say something along those lines when Mrs Radcliffe glances over my shoulder. When I turn around, Dad is standing in the doorway. I'm relieved to see he has some trousers on and, apart from the stubble and slightly crazy hair, he looks fairly normal. But there's something wrong – his face is clenched with rage and his eyes are burning with such ferocity I can't look at them.

There's only one reason Dad would look like that.

He's found out about the surprise. But how could he?

I look around for Celia but she's still in the kitchen.

When I turn back, Dad is barging into the room, pushing his way through the crowd, heading for the stereo. He grabs my phone and fumbles with the controls for a few seconds, only Dad's not so great with technology. I guess he's trying to turn it off, but instead the music suddenly booms out and everyone twitches like an electric charge just passed through the carpet. Eventually Dad yanks the wire out and the music stops with a loud pop.

He turns round and I'm sure he's going to shout at me. *How could I? Her favourite song! What was I thinking?* Then he notices everyone in the room is staring at him.

Dad coughs and puts my phone back on top of the stereo, then he looks at Mrs Radcliffe. 'Is it time?'

'Whenever you're ready,' she says with a thin smile.

I wait for Dad to move away from the stereo, then grab my phone. I've got to find Celia. We've got to stop it! If Dad reacted like that to me playing Mum's favourite song, he's going to lose it completely when he finds out what we've done.

Luckily, Celia is alone in the kitchen.

'You've got to call someone,' I blurt out. 'Tell them it's off! Dad's going to hate it.'

Celia puts down her bag and places her hands on my shoulders. 'We're doing this for your mum, Mina.' Her eyes lock on to mine. 'Your dad will understand. If he doesn't. . .' She sighs and shrugs. 'Today is for your mum – remember that.' She gives my shoulders a squeeze, then pulls me into her soft and substantial bosom.

'Come on, Mina, we're waiting.' Dad is in the doorway, his face pale as the paintwork.

Celia gives me a final hug and winks as she lets me go, but it does nothing to quell the shaking that has spread from my knees and is slowly taking over my entire body.

Where are you, Mum? I can't do this on my own!

I don't want to step through the front door. That's the signal. The moment they see us, a member of Celia's special squad waiting outside will make the call and everything we planned will begin.

I wonder if I've got time to run ahead? If I stand in the middle of the street so they can see me. . .

Then what? Is there a universal signal for *Oh my God, I've made a terrible mistake! Abort! Abort! Abort!*?

Dad links his arm through mine and the moment's gone. We're already moving towards the rectangle of outside framed in the doorway. One of the Dark Queen's attendants is waiting like a giant crow on the doorstep, a black umbrella flapping over his head, ready to protect us from the rain scratching lines through the air.

I shake my head. I want to feel the rain on my face – to feel the cold sting of it against my skin – anything to distract me from what is about to happen. But the man shadows us anyway. I wade through a puddle just to make a point. The cold water makes me shiver as it seeps into my shoes.

Mrs Radcliffe's deathmobile is parked at the kerb, its black paintwork and chrome shining out under the bruised sky. I can see the pale wooden box through the glass, almost buried by flowers: white roses from Dad and *MUM* spelt out in red carnations from me.

I imagine you beyond the wood, lying there alone in the dark. Cold. Stiff. Dead.

Fortunately gone.

Another monstrous vehicle waits for us, its doors held open by more shadowy attendants, their beady eyes tracking us from the house. Then I see the other cars, parked in every available space along the street, their paintwork bright and garish by comparison.

We're halfway between the house and the car. Each step is one closer to the bomb I set to go off. Dad must be able to feel me pulling back because he looks at me, the skin stretched taut around his jaw. I can see it would be too much for him to speak, but his eyes tell me: *Come on, Mina. We can do this, together.*

And then he hears it.

Dad's ears, always tuned in, hear it before anyone else.

The distant rumble of brass, the thump of a drum. . .

Dad stops walking and that's when Mrs Radcliffe registers the noise. The furry fiend above her eyes gathers itself into a query as her head jerks round. This wasn't on the schedule.

People start getting out of their cars, turning towards the sound coming from the bank of grey cloud obscuring the top of the hill.

And then we see them, materialising from the mist, five abreast in their green and gold jackets, marching down the centre of the road. Their instruments glisten in the rain, blasting a path through the damp and the cold while the Thackett Mill Brass Band banner flies proud above their heads.

The music is like a familiar voice calling out to me. I get the urge to run inside the house and fetch my trumpet – it feels wrong to not be a part of it. But I stand my ground, letting my fingers twitch over the invisible valves of the ghost instrument in my hands.

Does Dad feel it too? That he should be up there, in his rightful place leading the band?

I'm scared to look at him but force myself to do it.

Dad hasn't moved or spoken since the first echoes rolled out of the sky. His face is rigid, staring towards the sound while tears flood down his cheeks.

Then it hits me: the reason Dad turned his back on the band, on something that has been so much a part of him all his life. Why couldn't I see it before?

The band, this music – it's him and you, Mum. You're in every note. It's what brought you together in the first place, as teenagers, in a musty community hall. Your entire lives are here, written out across the staves. Dots and squiggles on a page, vibrations in the air to anyone else – but to Dad they are the beats of his heart, his very soul tossed naked into the rain for everyone to see.

How could I do this to him? In front of all these people.

As arranged, the people who have been waiting in their cars join the procession as it makes its way towards us, and suddenly I remember what comes next. Sure enough, before I can move or say anything, the band switches effortlessly into 'Hawaii Five-O', and Mrs Radcliffe's mouth falls open in a perfect circle of surprise.

Nobody other than you could have persuaded Dad to introduce cheesy TV themes into the band's repertoire, Mum. The crowds loved it, of course, and Dad had to admit you were right. But this isn't a summer fete or a concert in the park, this is a funeral! What have I done?

Finally Dad turns to me.

'Did you do this?' he demands, the words dragged from his throat, smothered in tears and snot.

I nod, losing the battle to stem the flood from my own eyes.

People at the back of the procession are clapping in time, and front doors are opening all along the street as neighbours come out of their houses to see what's going on. The air is filled with music and colour and celebration. And suddenly I'm not sorry any more. This is what you wanted.

'I did it for Mum,' I say, and for once my voice holds.

Dad's eye blaze into mine, fierce and unreadable, blurred by both our tears.

Then he grabs me and pulls me to him.

'Perfect.' The word is buried in my hair but I still hear it. 'Bloody brilliant!' He steps back, staring into my face. 'You're your mother's daughter all right!' he says, almost having to shout to be heard above the band. 'She would have bloody loved this, Mina! Bloody loved it!'

Then he smiles – actually smiles! I realise how long it is since I last saw that.

Dad turns to Mrs Radcliffe who is still gaping like a fish.

'What are you waiting for?' he says. 'You lead, we'll follow.'

He grabs my hand and we walk past the waiting car and join the head of the procession. Celia is already there and she takes hold of my other hand.

We march to the crematorium, the deathmobile out in front and your band playing every step of the way.

And you're not inside that box, Mum, you're here – in the music, in every smile, beside every person walking with us, singing and laughing.

You'll always be here.

Bodies wear out, get ill and die, but you were more than just a body. I don't believe in God, or an afterlife, or any of that stuff – but I believe there is life after death. Because you are a part of all the people you ever met. You live on in our memories, your stories, the things you taught us – like how to make magpie soup. I realise now that we are each our own magpie soup: a crazy, unique, brilliant mix of all the people we love and the things we do.

We won't ever stop loving you or missing having you to hold, but we'll be OK. Because you are part of us. Not even death can take that away.

NIGHTLIGHT

by Sara Grant

Usually noise keeps me company at night. Alex snores a little. Josey mumbles in her sleep. Momma giggles when a boyfriend stays over. Crickets hum in the tall grass. Trucks rumble down the highway. Sometimes I hear breakin' glass or shoutin', but it don't bother me much. Tonight I hear voices. Momma, her new boyfriend and the neighbours from across the way are huddled round the kitchen table, drinkin' coffee and talkin'. Talkin' about me, I suspect.

Words float from the kitchen like lost balloons at the county fair, except I'm the one who's cryin' like some two-year-old, reachin' skyward like I could snatch today back. One phrase gets stuck like Momma's scratched Elvis record. 'Hell and fire.' 'Hell and fire.' 'Hell and fire.' I wonder if that's my punishment and my eternal restin' place.

I focus on the swirls in the trailer's wood panellin' and count the number of pink flowers on the wallpaper. I squint and read all the book titles on the bookcase Momma and I put together. It leans a little to the left but it's OK.

The nightlight smoothes the rough edges in my room. Momma insisted on a nightlight. I told her I wasn't no baby. I hate the stupid thing. Josey and Alex bawl like babies if I switch it off, but I like lyin' in the pitch black and lettin' my mind wander. The time I hid it, Momma anned my hide. When she found it in the shoebox with those stupid patent leather shoes she makes me wear on Sundays, I told her I was the oldest so I should get to decide about nightlights.

'Helen Friar,' she said. 'Helen Friar, you are the oldest so you should want to protect Josey and Alex. They get scared of the dark.' Momma always uses both my names when I'm in trouble. It's like that Martin Luther King, Jr. feller that was killed a few months back. No one ever called him Marty or nothin' and it seems he was always stirrin' up trouble.

Well, I told Momma I wasn't scared, and I ain't – not of spiders or even Old Miss Anderson with the glass eye. But tonight it's as if I can feel the flames of hell lickin' at my backside. My insides are all bunched up. I'm squirmin' in my bed like a firefly trapped in a jelly jar. I want to erase today. Call for a 'do-over' like in gym class. But right now that just don't seem possible.

Today was the kind of hot summer day that your only choices are meltin' or swimmin' – unless you are a Dawson or Taylor, cause then you'd have air conditionin' and TV. The countryside had opened up and vomited kids right in the blue chlorinated water. There was barely one foot of space on the cement for a towel, or room in that water to splash properly. Jenna and me scooted over a few rainbow-striped towels that I'd seen on special at the Dollar General Store last summer.

We never came to the pool together before. I liked to swim laps, seeing as I won the city junior swim championships three years runnin'. She wanted to sunbathe. She didn't like to get her hair wet, she said. She wore her hair in six pigtails, each twisted like a rope.

I had to beg Momma to let Jenna borrow her new red swimsuit. Jenna had developed before any of the rest of us. She was a foot taller than me and a bit skinnier but other than that we were the same in all the important ways. We liked orange soda pop and Paul Newman, and we both were gonna be movie stars and everybody in this dinky town would drive all the way to Indianapolis to see our shows. In that red swimsuit with all those new curves and the brown glow of her black skin, she looked the part already.

Jenna and me had been best friends since November when her family moved from Mississippi into the trailer next to mine. I asked her once why in tarnation would someone want to move to Indiana. Mississippi had a river and beaches and way more sunshine. She said I wasn't black so I couldn't understand. Whatever that meant. My momma always said colour don't matter. Jenna pointed out it was easy to say colour don't matter when everyone is white.

Today at the pool the sun was bakin' me from the top, and the cement was grillin' my backside. I told Jenna I needed a soda if we weren't gonna swim. I hopped and skipped on the balls of my feet as quick as I could to keep from burnin' my skin plum off.

When I came back, I couldn't find Jenna at first. She wasn't that hard to spot in the red suit and her being the only black girl in town and all. I didn't have to guess what had happened. Our stuff was all bunched in a ball and the rainbow towels were spread out nice and long where ours had been. Two older boys had hold of Jenna and were pushin' and pullin' her like she was the rope in tug o' war. The names they called her, I'll never forget and never ever repeat. Minutes before you could hardly see the water for the bobbin' heads but now a big patch of blue had opened up.

Jenna wasn't just screamin' her head off like some scaredy girl in a monster movie. She was yellin' somethin' specific. She was yellin' my name over and over and makin' it twist together into new words.

'Helen Friar.'

'Helenfriar.'

'Hell and fire.'

'Hell and fire.'

It wasn't that I froze exactly. It wasn't that I was scared or nothin'. My brain instead of thinkin' of Jenna was thinkin' of me. I watched as they made her a human slingshot and launched her into the pool.

They said 'accident'. The two lifeguards on duty swear they tried, but I saw one of them snap the cap on her suntan oil and the other carefully remove his sunglasses before they jumped in. Kids drown in that pool at least once a summer. But none of them had a friend who won the city junior swim championship three years runnin'.

Now I lie in bed perfectly still. My nightgown is bunched around my waist and pasted with sweat to my body. I replay the afternoon, and this time I stand up. This time I step in. This time Jenna and I walk away and share my orange soda. 'Helen Friar,' she'd say. 'Helen Friar, you're all right.'

I close my eyes for a second. The minute the darkness creeps in I see Jenna and her red swimsuit tyin' herself in knots tryin' to get out of that water. How was I supposed to know she couldn't swim?

My eyelids pop open. In the glow of the nightlight, I look hard for somethin' else to see. Alex suckin' his thumb. Josey's face smushed against her pillow. My three swimmin' trophies on the top of the bookcase with their tiny, gold, plastic swimmers preparin' to dive head first into darkness.

TRICK OR TWEET?

by Katie Dale

I round the street corner and freeze. The party is already heaving, witches and wizards and werewolves spilling out onto the damp front lawn as music blares from inside the house.

I take a deep breath, trying to slow my racing heartbeat.

All these people.

All these strangers.

I grit my teeth to steady my nerves, forcing one foot in front of the other.

You can do this, man. You can. You've been planning it for ages. This is your chance. You bought a freaking costume and everything, for goodness' sake – you're not wimping out now!

So there are more people than I'd thought. But that's good, in a way. It makes it easier.

And harder.

I scan everyone's faces as I walk up the driveway, but I can't see her. I don't recognise anybody. Not yet. But I guess that's kind of the point of a masquerade party. I adjust my own mask as I edge past the throng to the front door, but it's even more rammed inside, and it's hot – too hot. My pulse races as sweat trickles between my shoulder blades – it's getting hard to breathe. . .

Water. I need water.

I squeeze my way through the crowded hallway, searching for the kitchen.

Lounge. . . Dining room. . . Conservatory. . .

Finally I find the kitchen, push my way to the sink, grab a glass and fill it from the tap. I down it in one.

'Oh my god, *another Batman!*'

I turn to see a girl in a Catwoman costume rushing towards me and my heart stops.

Is it her?

'I have *got* to get a selfie with you!' she squeals, pulling a mobile phone from a glittery bag. 'Do you mind?'

There's no time to reply as she flings her arm over my shoulder and her phone flashes in my face.

She checks the screen. 'Fabulous! What's your Twitter handle?'

I stare at her dumbly.

'What's the matter? Cat got your tongue?' She winks. 'Not yet – we've only just met!'

She laughs and I feel my cheeks burn. Thank goodness I'm wearing a mask.

'Just teasing.' She flutters her eyelashes at me. 'What's your Twitter name? I'll tweet you.'

'Um, I'm not on Twitter,' I lie.

She stares at me. 'Seriously? Wow, I thought *everyone* was! My entire *life*'s online! Have we met?'

'Um, no.'

'I thought not. I swear I've never seen half these people before in my life – who knew Jen had so many friends? I mean, she's so quiet at school and she only has, like, twenty followers on Twitter!'

I frown. So what?

'So anyway, I'm Georgia.'

I know.

'And you are. . .?'

'Um . . . Bruce.'

'No way! For real?' She laughs. 'Well at least you have a cool excuse for your outfit, then. Apart from witches and wizards, Batman seems to be the Halloween theme *du jour*.' She gestures around the room. 'Though most of the guys have gone for Joker costumes. Sick, huh? I've counted at least three other Catwomen, though. Ugh. Irritating.'

'Really? Where?' I look around.

'Well, there are two over there.' She points through the door at two girls I don't recognise in the dining room. 'Plus I saw one in the back garden earlier. Probably hiding.'

I frown again. 'Why?'

'Well, the lighting's a bit harsh in here.' She lowers her voice conspiratorially. 'And to be honest the Lycra leggings weren't doing her any favours. Yikes.'

Wow. It's not just her costume that's catty.

'Ooh! I love this song!' Georgia cries as a new tune blasts out of the sound system. 'Do you wanna dance?'

'Actually, I'm dying for the loo,' I say, edging away. 'All that water.'

'OK. Well, come find me later!' As she shimmies away, I breathe a sigh of relief.

I down another glass of water, then head out the back door into the cool night air.

The garden is decorated in tiny twinkling fairy lights, and filled with dark costumed figures. How is anyone meant to ever recognise anyone else at these parties? Or maybe they're not? Maybe it's all about being anonymous. Safety in the shadows.

I can relate to that.

I keep my head down as I weave through the clusters of people. Then, as I cross the patio, I spot another Catwoman sitting alone on the garden wall, her masked face illuminated by the glow from her smartphone.

It's her.

Chloe.

I take a deep breath, swallow hard, and walk over.

'Nice necklace, Selina,' I say, in my best Christian Bale/Batman voice.

'Selina?' She frowns, then smiles. 'Oh, right! Um . . . thank you, Mr Wayne.'

'Very *Breakfast at Tiffany's*,' I add, nodding at her pearls.

She laughs. 'That's my favourite film!'

I know.

'No way.' I smile. 'Me too.'

'Really?' She raises an eyebrow. 'You must be the first guy I've met who's even *seen* it.'

'Are you kidding?' I scoff. 'It's a classic! That bit where Audrey Hepburn sings "Moon River" on the fire escape?'

'Awesome.' She nods. 'But it's the bit with the cat at the end that really gets me.'

'In the rain?'

'Yes!'

'Ugh!' I shake my head. 'Blatant audience manipulation.'

'I know – but it works!'

'Tell me about it. Makes me cry every time.'

'It does not!' She giggles.

'Like a baby.' I nod ruefully.

She laughs, a rich, full, carefree sound, then smiles up at me. 'I'm Chloe.'

I know.

I sit down next to her on the wall. 'Bruce.'

'Yeah, right.' She rolls her eyes.

I shrug. 'What's in a name, right?'

'Oh god, your favourite film's *Breakfast at Tiffany's*, and now you're quoting *Romeo and Juliet* at me? Are you for real?'

I shrug again.

Her mobile phone suddenly lights up and she looks down at the screen as a photo of a grinning group of girls appears.

'Are they your friends?' I ask, though I already know they're her #BFFs: Kim, Lara and Stacey.

But to my surprise it's her turn to shrug.

'We kinda fell out.'

'Why?'

She shakes her head. 'It's silly.'

'I doubt it. You wouldn't be upset if it was silly.'

She smiles. 'You don't even know me.'

If only she knew.

Georgia was right, people's whole lives are online now, and I know more about Chloe – aka @Chlover – than any other girl I've ever met, even though this is the first time we've actually spoken.

And that's not a coincidence.

'So what happened?' I ask.

'There's this guy I like. Ryan.'

My heart sinks. She didn't put *that* online.

'But ten minutes after we got here someone tweeted a photo of Lara – that's the girl in the witch outfit – kissing him.'

'Ouch.' I saw that tweet. It didn't look like a kiss so much as like Lara was trying to eat him alive.

'She says I'm overreacting.' Chloe sighs. 'That it was just a stupid kiss at a party and it didn't mean anything – and it probably doesn't. Not to her. She can have anyone she wants. Even if she doesn't really want them.'

I frown. Lara doesn't sound much like a BFF to me – unless it stands for Bitchy Fake Friend.

'So that's why you're out here and she's in there?' I ask.

'Yeah, having the time of her life by the looks of it.' Chloe looks sadly at Lara's photo. 'Actually, do you mind if I tweet a picture of us?'

'Not at all.' I lean in as she holds the phone at arm's length.

A photo of me with Chloe.

On Twitter.

Just yesterday I would've been over the moon, but something niggles at me as she shows me the picture now. There's no trace of sadness in the photo she's broadcasting to the world. It's the same confident, carefree, fun-loving smile I've seen a hundred times online. But if it's not real now . . . how often does she fake it? And why is she tweeting it? Because Lara posted a photo of herself having a good time? Is that how it works? A constant contest to prove who's having the most fun?

'Thanks.' Chloe smiles at me as she slides her phone back into her bag. 'You probably think I'm beyond pathetic, right?'

'Not at all.'

'I should never have come tonight,' she sighs. 'This is *so* not my scene.'

'What, parties?' But she's got dozens of party photos on her Twitter feed. . .

'They're such an effort!' she groans. 'Small talk, crowds of people, deafening music, blah blah blah. Give me a good book and a comfy chair any day. Boring, huh?'

It's my turn to smile. 'Not at all.' Sounds perfect.

'And I can't believe I dressed up – in Lycra of all things! Lycra! With my legs! And all because Ryan's favourite movie is *The Dark Knight* and I knew he was coming as the Joker.' She rolls her eyes. 'How lame is that?'

I shift uncomfortably. 'Not *that* lame. . .'

'I don't even like the new Batman films.' She glances at my costume. 'No offence.'

'Me neither,' I confess, truthfully. 'Give me Tim Burton any day.'

'Me too!' She grins. '*The Dark Knight*'s too dark and broody for me. And Michelle Pfeiffer was SO much better than Anne Hathaway.'

'Definitely.' I laugh. 'But you know who would've made a great Catwoman?'

'Who?'

'Audrey Hepburn.'

'Totally! You know, Adam Hughes based his—'

'Catwoman covers on Audrey Hepburn,' I finish with her, and she laughs in surprise.

'You knew that?' Her eyes twinkle in the moonlight.

'I read it somewhere.' I grin, amazed that *she* knows it.

'I'm a bit of a closet comic-book geek,' Chloe confesses. 'Don't tell anyone.'

'I won't.' I wink, thrilled that we actually have more in common that I ever thought possible. 'Besides, I bet I can out-geek you.'

'Uh, unlikely!' she scoffs. 'Unless you can name all the DC characters you won't even come close.'

I raise an eyebrow. 'How about all the DC *and* Marvel characters?'

'Ooh, game on!' She laughs and I grin. She's even better in real life.

'You know, I'm actually kinda glad I came tonight after all.' She beams at me and my skin tingles. Is this actually happening? Does she feel it too. . .?

Suddenly there's a yell and a scream and the sound of breaking glass and we both turn in time to see a group of guys barrel out of the kitchen door and land in a sprawling mess of flying fists on the lawn.

Talk about ruining the moment.

'Stop it!' a girl in a black fairy costume screams at them. 'Stop, or I'll call the police!'

Chloe jumps to her feet. 'Jen, what's happening? Who are those guys?'

'I don't know!' the fairy girl cries. 'I don't know half the people here – they're gatecrashers!'

'*Gatecrashers*?' Chloe gasps.

I turn away quickly before Jen realises I'm one too.

'They've drunk all my dad's whisky and smashed my mum's antique vase!' Jen wails.

'I'm calling the police.' Chloe grabs her mobile from her bag. 'You hear that, everyone? Anyone who wasn't invited, get out now! The police will be here soon!'

Uh-oh.

'Sounds like they're already here,' someone says as the wail of sirens pierces the air.

I freeze. The fighting guys scramble past each other in their hurry to leave and I look at Chloe, torn. I don't want to go, not now, when we're getting on better than I ever dreamed, but if Jen spots me she'll know I gatecrashed and Chloe will never want to see me again.

Plus, I could get arrested.

'I'm gonna head home,' I tell Chloe.

'Already?' She frowns.

'Yeah – I've got a strict curfew, plus the party will be over anyway, once the police are here.'

'True.' She sighs.

'Can I . . . can I walk you home?' I offer hopefully.

'I can't – I should stay and make sure Jen's OK.'

I nod. 'Well, it was . . . it was really great to meet you.'

She smiles. 'You too, Bruce. See you around!'

But will she? Tomorrow I'll be back to being invisible. She doesn't know my real name. Or even what I look like.

I sigh as I walk through the garden gate and turn the corner.

That was it. That was my chance.

And now it's over.

But as I pull out my own phone and open Twitter, there we are – the two of us, beaming at the camera.

I smile.

That's something.

'Bruce!' someone calls, and I freeze. 'Bruce! Wait!'

I turn to see her wobbling on her high heels as she runs towards me and my heart lifts.

'I thought you had to stay?'

'Jen had a whole crowd round her,' she says with a shrug. 'Drama attracts friends! Plus the party's over anyway, it's dark, I'm dressed ridiculously, and who better to escort me through the mean streets of

Worthing than a caped crusader?'

I grin, hold out my arm and put on my best Batman growl. 'My pleasure, ma'am.'

'Why thank you, kind sir.' She grins, linking her arm through mine. 'Now, I believe we were about to have a comic-book geek-off. . .'

I laugh.

As we walk along the dark streets comparing our favourite superheroes and villains it's like we've known each other for ages. I knew we'd get on like a house on fire given half a chance. Everything's working out even better than I planned.

'What time's your curfew?' Chloe asks eventually. 'I don't want to make you late.'

'Don't worry,' I say. 'Mayflower Lane's on my way home.'

Chloe stops walking. 'What?'

'I go right past it – it's no trouble.'

She lets go of my arm. 'Bruce . . . I never told you I live on Mayflower Lane.'

I freeze.

She backs away from me. 'How did you know that?'

'Chloe. . .'

'*How did you know?*' she demands. 'Have you been *stalking* me?'

'No!' I protest. 'Not stalking – researching!'

Her eyebrows shoot upwards. '*Researching?* What does that even mean? How did you know where I live?'

'I. . .' I sigh. I don't want to lie to her. Besides, I can't think of a convincing excuse. 'Twitter.'

'*Twitter?*' She stares at me. 'I've never put my address on Twitter!'

'Well, no . . . but you've posted photos, details. . .'

'Details?' Her eyes widen. 'Such as?'

I bite my lip.

'Oh my God.' She pulls out her phone quickly.

'Chloe, please.' I step towards her, but she backs away.

'Don't come near me!' she warns, scrolling down her screen. 'Oh my

God, that's how you knew I was going to be at the party – and what I'd be wearing. Is that why you dressed as *Batman*?'

I nod helplessly.

'But how did you find my house just from a few photos?'

'The same way I found Jen's.' I sigh. 'Google Street View – you just need the area and a few photos, and—'

'Oh my God, *you gatecrashed the party too*?' Her jaw drops. 'Do you even *know* Jen?'

'I. . .' I hesitate, then shake my head.

'You're such a *creep*!' she screams, turning and running away down the dark street.

'No! Chloe! Wait!' I protest. 'I can explain!'

But it's no good. She keeps running. And I don't blame her.

I've blown it.

Then suddenly her ankle twists and she topples to the pavement.

'Chloe!' I rush towards her. 'Chloe, are you OK?'

'Back off!' she cries, scrambling to her feet, but her ankle collapses again and she stumbles. 'Stupid heels!'

'Chloe, it's dark, you're hurt – at least let me help you home.' I take her hand, but she snatches it away.

'Stay away from me! I mean it. I'll phone the police!'

I sigh and back away. 'Well, let me call you a taxi then – please?'

'I can call my own freaking taxi.' She scowls. She perches on a garden wall, pulls out her phone and punches the numbers violently. She asks for a cab, then frowns at the phone. 'What do you mean it's going to be an hour?' she moans. 'Never mind.' She hangs up and sighs heavily.

I swallow hard. 'Could your parents pick you up?'

'No. Mum works nights.'

'What about your dad?'

She shakes her head and I frown. Her dad's still around – I've seen photos of him, a happy, smiley man. 'Why not?'

'Because . . . because he'll be passed out drunk by now,' she says quietly. 'As usual.'

I swallow hard. Wow. No wonder he was so smiley. . .

'I'll just have to walk.' She pushes herself off the wall and winces as her foot touches the ground.

'Chloe, you can't walk – not by yourself. You're hurt.'

'I'll manage.'

'Please,' I beg. 'You never have to see me again, just . . . let me help you get home safely.'

She hesitates, tests her foot again, then sighs. 'Fine.'

I hurry over and put my arm around her shoulders, taking her weight.

We walk in silence for a few minutes. I'm scared to speak in case I make things worse.

If that's even possible.

'I can't believe you found out all that just from the internet.' she says eventually. 'Why did you do it? And why me?'

'Because . . . Chloe, you're amazing.' I sigh. 'I see you every day at school and I've wanted to talk to you a million times, but . . . you're so completely out of my league, you don't even know I exist and I'm . . . I'm shy.' I confess, feeling my cheeks burn painfully, but I need to explain, need her to understand – and this is probably the only chance I'll ever get. 'I'm not good with girls. I always get . . . tongue-tied and say stupid things and I knew if I tried to talk to you I'd just totally mess it up. But I wanted to get to know you better, so I followed you on Twitter. The more I saw, the more I liked you – you're so sweet and funny and popular and pretty – and it made me want to meet you even more . . . but you only get one chance to make a first impression so I . . . I did some research – *lots* of research – to try to make sure it went well.'

'Kinda backfired,' she mutters.

'I know. I'm sorry,' I say miserably. 'I just wanted you to like me.'

'I did like you,' Chloe says quietly. 'I really enjoyed talking to you tonight. We seemed to have so much in common, it was unreal.' She sighs. 'But it *was* unreal. It was all lies. You're not the person I thought you were.'

'Well, you're not the person I thought you were, either,' I counter. 'You're not the confident social butterfly you make yourself out to be online, you don't have the perfect friends and family and life you seemed to. . .'

She opens her mouth to protest, then frowns and closes it again.

'Why do you pretend?'

She shrugs. 'I don't know. I want people to like me, I guess.'

'But people would like you. The real you.'

She gives me a wry smile. 'You don't know the real me.'

'I know you're a closet comic-book geek, that you hate wearing high heels, don't like parties, and would rather spend an evening curled up with a good book.'

She bites her lip.

'All of which makes me like you,' I say. 'And I'd love to get to know you better. The real you.'

'But I don't know who you are.' She looks up at me sadly. 'Was anything you said tonight true?'

I take a deep breath. Here goes. . . 'I *am* a comic-book geek, I do prefer the Tim Burton Batman films, and I really, really hate parties and would *much* prefer to stay at home.'

She raises an eyebrow.

'But . . . *Breakfast at Tiffany's* isn't my favourite film – I'd never even seen it before last week, and to be honest it was a bit of a yawn. . .'

'Whatever.' She looks away.

'But it did make me cry.'

Her mouth twitches.

'Like a baby.'

She smiles.

'And I really, really, hate dressing up – especially wearing a freaking mask.'

'Then take it off,' she says.

I hesitate, and she leans forward and gently takes it off, then removes her own.

As we stand face to face for the first time, I bite my lip. She is even more beautiful than her online photos.

But I want to run.

I feel exposed.

I feel vulnerable.

I feel terrified.

But she doesn't cringe or wince or run away.

Instead, she takes my hand.

'Harry.' She smiles.

My heart stops. 'You know who I am?'

'Not yet.' She says, squeezing my hand. 'Not really. But I'd like to.'

And as I help her home I cannot stop the stupid smile splitting my face.

Aladdin's Lamp

by Savita Kalhan

Priti's heart fluttered and her hands were all fingers and thumbs as she loaded the tray with her family's best china. Rimmed with a band of gold, the tea set was a precious family heirloom and had only made its appearance three times before in Priti's memory. The silver cutlery shone as though it had been rubbed as many times as Aladdin's lamp, but unlike the boy's in the tale, Priti's wishes remained unanswered. At school, she had been studying the origins of fairy stories, and when her teacher, Mrs Bandar, told the class that Aladdin was actually Chinese, no one believed her.

'Look it up for yourselves,' she said. 'Things are not always what they seem.'

So Priti went home and looked it up on Wikipedia – and there it was in black and white: Aladdin was Chinese. Walt Disney had got it wrong, or at least it had all gone wrong somewhere along the chain from the telling and the writing of the story, the translations it had gone through, and all the subsequent retellings, until its most recent animated incarnation. It seemed that a man from Syria had originally recounted the tale to a Frenchman named Antoine Galland, who had then simply added it to his collection of stories, *One Thousand and One Arabian Nights*, published in 1710. He did the same with the stories of 'Ali Baba and the Forty Thieves' and 'Sinbad the Sailor'.

So Mrs Bandar was right. If you retell a tale enough times, you can change important details and people will still believe it.

But Priti did not care whether Aladdin was Arabian, Persian or Chinese: she just wished the story were true. Today, of all days, she needed a magic lamp.

The man sitting in the other room, alongside his uncle, had started telling tall tales almost as soon as he had walked through the door. Priti did not believe any of them, not a single word of the many tales he had told rang true. But it was his manner – that arrogance of someone who feels they are entitled to something by right, the overbearing confidence, the laugh that needed to fill the whole room, and the sloping eyes that slipped and slid this way and that but invariably came to settle on her – that troubled her most.

No, actually what troubled her most was that her parents were so completely taken in by him.

Priti pushed open the kitchen door with her foot, the tray carefully balanced in her hands, and walked through to the living room, wondering how, in the days before the internet laid open any secret you cared to uncover, people ever got to the truth. She thought she knew the answer – they didn't, not unless they really wanted to. Discovering the truth required one to probe deeper, to make checks and ask lots of questions of other people. Most people probably would not have bothered to go to such lengths. A recommendation, a word from a trusted go-between or a distant relation would have been enough. For her parents, still stuck in the last century, this was how it still was.

But it certainly wasn't like that for her.

In the time it had taken for the kettle to boil, Priti had googled him on her phone, her fingers flying across the keypad. So she knew all she needed to know about him.

'America is a great country,' her father was saying. 'Not like here in India. Once we were a great nation, but no longer. Priti is doing well at school, top of her class. This is her final year – she will take honours, I know. She works hard, very hard. She wants to go to college and then to university, but there are plenty of universities in America! She can go there – until the children come, of course.' Her father laughed. Her mother smiled. Priti forced herself not to cringe.

'But she is an excellent cook, also,' her mother added. 'Her chapattis are as thin as rice paper and as light as the air we breathe. And of course, she speaks English as though it was her mother tongue, not Punjabi!'

'But she is a simple girl at heart and not too modern – not like some of the girls these days. Oh, but she is not backward in any way, no, I do not mean that,' her father hastily corrected himself.

She set the tray of clinking cups and saucers, a steaming pot of tea, sugar bowl and milk jug on the coffee table and poured the tea. It was as though she was not in the room, was merely a phantom, a figment of their imagination. But she feared this man before her *had* no imagination.

She had been told his name, that he worked for a bank, that he lived in Chicago, and that he had been a bachelor all these years so that he could further his career and be in a better position when he married. He said he had a flat in the city. He had no family close by. He had a brother who emigrated to Australia, but had not been able to visit him because it was so, so far, and his parents had died a long time ago. His uncle lived in India, but in a little village conveniently far away from their town.

That was all she had been told. But it was enough.

It was enough for her parents too. They were too hasty, her parents, far hastier than she. It surprised her. She knew they loved her and wanted nothing but the best for her. She was the last child of the family, the baby, the last daughter unwed. They wanted something better for her, they said. She was ten years younger than her nearest sibling, her brother, and almost twenty years younger than her eldest sister. She was a late arrival, but the one they wanted to send the furthest.

She took her place beside her mother, and slipped her arm through the older woman's. For some reason her mother seemed to think that the slight, twitchy suitor seated before them was worthy of her getting out all her finery. So today she was aglow in gold, and even her deep burgundy silk sari was lavishly embroidered with gold thread. Priti knew that her mother was stifling under the weight of it all for there was a fine sheen of perspiration on her face. The ceiling fan was on the highest setting but it was simply pushing the humid air around the room.

Her parents believed that the reason she did not want to live so far away was because they were aging and would need someone to take care of them. The truth was far more complicated than that, but it was a truth that could never be spoken out loud. She could never find the words, not in Punjabi and not in English, and sometimes she could barely even say the words inside her own head. They were words that in some families would bring on an unfortunate accident and an untimely death. In truth, she was unsure what would happen in her own family. Words that are unspoken cannot be repeated and cannot be held against anyone.

He was looking at her again. She shifted uncomfortably in the face of his open scrutiny, suddenly conscious of the damp patch under her arms, the trickle of sweat rolling down between her breasts. Her outfit was her mother's choice but neither of them had accounted for the sudden heat wave. February was not known to be a blisteringly hot month. It was a month when the quilts were normally brought out as the sun dipped below the horizon, and as night deepened the fireplace flickered and danced with darting tongues of orange flames. Priti loved February just for that reason.

'What will you do?' her best friend Jyoti had asked her.

That was only just yesterday. For Priti it felt as though a millions years had since passed.

She'd snuggled closer to her friend under the quilt. Jyoti had secured a place at the girls' college when school finished. She wasn't being forced into marriage and shipped off to a place that held only the promise of countless years of loneliness.

'We could run away,' Priti had suggested.

'Priti, you know I can't do that.' Her friend's tone had a finality to it. The rest was left unsaid.

Jyoti did have plans, plans that did not involve staying in their little town, or even staying in the country. She would go to college for two years, then university for three years, after which she would inevitably graduate with a first-class degree in Maths, and then find a job abroad. She would fend for herself, bask in her independence and her freedom – freedom to do as she pleased; freedom to live the way she wanted to live; freedom to love whomever she wanted to love. Nothing would hold her back as nothing meant more to her, not her family and certainly not her best friend. Losing Priti was a high price to pay but Jyoti was prepared to pay it for her freedom.

They hadn't spoken today. They might never speak again, Priti realised. It would be too painful for them both.

What price would Priti pay for freedom?

RP ('as they fondly call me over there in the great US of A') was recounting yet another story. This one was about RP, the unifier of communities. The previous one had been about RP, the founder of a charity helping homeless kids. Before that it was how RP, through sheer hard work and dedication, became the youngest ever manager in his major-league bank.

He wasn't that young. He claimed to be thirty-one but he looked much older. His hair was thinning, the hairline receding, but he laughed it away with assured ease. 'It comes to us Patels early. There is no space for hair with our brains so bursting with thoughts and ideas and ambition. Oh yes, we are an ambitious lot. And look where it has got us! To America, the land of the free, where your dreams can come true.' He slapped his thighs with his hands. 'Yes, my dreams have come true. Well, all except one, that is.' His sloping eyes glanced at Priti in such a meaningful way that both her parents and his uncle seemed to feel compelled to look at her too.

Priti was trying desperately hard not to retch. She lowered her eyes, but then fearing that he might misread this as demureness, she raised them again and stared back at him, expressionless. He looked away first. She felt the sharp stab of her mother's elbow in her side, admonishing her to drop her gaze. But she would not.

'So, Rajesh, when did you first go to America?' she asked him. It was practically the first thing she had said all afternoon so the surprised silence that ensued was not unexpected. 'What year was it?'

'Oh, many years ago now. I'm not counting. It has begun to feel so much like home. I do miss many things here, of course. The food, for example. One would think you could find a good Indian restaurant in the city. But no, not one of them serves the food one finds here on every street corner and in every house.'

She cut him off. 'So when was that?' she asked again.

He shrugged. 'It was so long ago that I can barely remember. But they bring all the latest films over there. Three Indian cinemas and every weekend they are full. You will not miss much, Priti.'

He still had not answered her question. 'I don't care for Bollywood films,' she said abruptly. She felt the elbow in her side again but ploughed on regardless. 'A complete waste of three hours of my life which I could have spent studying or reading. So when exactly did you move to the States?'

'After I graduated. The exams were extra tough that year, but somehow I came out with a top honours degree in Business Studies. What celebrations we had, all my family and friends so proud.'

'Of course they were proud of you,' her father said. 'It is a most excellent achievement.'

'So what year was that? Which university did you graduate from?

How long have you been in the States?' Priti probed again.

'Mumbai had the best Business degree in my time. It was very far from home, of course, and absolutely impossible for me to travel back to see my family because of the expense, but it was a sacrifice I had to make. We all have to make sacrifices. I know you, Uncleji and Auntyji, will understand what I mean,' he said to her mother and father.

'Yes, we know, *beta*,' her mother said with a heavy sigh. 'The young today do not understand the trouble their parents have gone to to ensure they want for nothing in life. It is our duty as parents to give them the best we can.'

'There are quite a few universities in Mumbai. Which one did you go to?' Priti asked. Her mum's use of *beta* disturbed her. RP was in no way like a son to her mum – and if Priti had anything to do with it, he never would be.

He smiled affably at her. 'The best one, of course!' He laughed too loud. 'So what is your best subject at school? What would you like to study at college?' He did not wait for her answer and had yet again managed to wriggle out of answering hers. 'There are many colleges in Chicago – you can take your pick! Your English may need a little more work even though it is very good, just as your parents have said,' he hastened to add. 'In America standards are higher than here, you understand. There may be entrance exams to sit, depending on the course you choose. You will only be offered a place should you do well in those exams. But you will be OK, Priti. Your parents have told me how you study very hard.'

How dare he! Her English was far better than his halting version, heavily accented and with the stresses in all the wrong places – it was obvious, surely? Hers was accented but only softly so. She had spent many hours listening to the BBC World Service to perfect it. She recorded herself and listened to the recordings. As for him, well, it sounded as though he had just gone over to America on the last boat. Surely after so many years there he should sound more American?

But he was clearly one of those people who enjoyed slanting things to his own advantage, playing on people's emotions to achieve his own ends. In this case, the people whose emotions he was playing on were her parents, easily manipulated when the stakes were high, and for them the stakes were very high today because they had deemed RP the most eligible prospective son-in-law to cross the threshold.

Priti had a big problem on her hands. Now sixteen, she had already been forced to see two other suitors before RP had landed in the living room. The first had come from the neighbouring city. She had quite liked him. He was two years older than her, had just finished college with no desire – translated by her parents as no money – to go to university. He was honest, nice looking, and had a quietly understated sense of humour. But he was not wealthy and neither did he have great prospects, at least as far as her parents were concerned. He worked in reception at a hotel, but he had just been put on the hotel's management trainee programme. The hotel, after closer quizzing, turned out to be part of an international hotel chain and, when Priti looked into it and into him, she realised that he actually had very good prospects but had downplayed them. It wasn't in his character to brag or make a show of himself.

Unlike the man sitting before her.

The second suitor had also been pleasant enough. He had studied to be a pharmacist and had just started work in the city. It seemed that his parents, sitting either side of him, were far keener that he marry than he was. 'He is so lonely, away from home, without his family, and he is anxious to start his new life with his wife by his side.'

Priti was beginning to wonder what was wrong with all the city girls that the men felt compelled to travel out to the smaller towns and villages for their brides. And just why were they looking for sixteen-year-old girls rather than ones closer to their own age? Did they think it would be easier to control them, order them about, keep them meek and subservient if they got them younger?

Did they not realise that a new age was dawning – that they would have to go further afield, to ever-smaller villages to find what they were looking for?

So far RP had managed to wriggle out of directly answering any of her questions. She began to doubt that in the end she would be able to show her parents what he really was. Even if she did manage it, it would not stop other suitors knocking on their door. It would not stop Jyoti leaving.

Priti's family meant the world to her and, unlike Jyoti, she could not bear to leave them to find the freedom that Jyoti so craved. They could carve out a future here, Priti had told her. There were many girls who remained unmarried.

'But I want to be who I am,' Jyoti had answered. 'And I cannot be that here. Neither can you.'

Priti needed a miracle. She needed an Aladdin's lamp with a genie who would grant her three wishes. She would have settled for just the one wish if that was the only choice.

But Aladdin's lamp was just another tall tale.

She had told Jyoti about the origins of the story. Jyoti was not a great reader like Priti, but even she had found hearing about the origins of the story interesting. A few days later she had presented Priti with a gift. 'Here, this is for you. I found it in the bazaar.' She handed Priti a small package wrapped in gold paper and tied with a red bow.

Priti opened it carefully. Jyoti was not a gift giver, and certainly never a spur-of-the-moment gift giver. Her birthday presents to Priti were always late but always thoughtful. Priti had wondered what could be inside the beautifully wrapped package.

'Why so slow, Priti? Tear it open!'

Priti ignored her friend and carefully unsealed the sticky tape holding the package together. The paper fell away to reveal a small oil lamp. Its brass was tarnished to a dull brown with no hint of its original glimmer or beauty. The top was sealed shut with rust. If there had ever been a genie inside, he would have perished long ago.

'Sorry, it's going to need a heck of a rubbing to find the genie hiding inside it,' Jyoti had said with a laugh. She hadn't meant it unkindly, but Priti felt as if Jyoti was mocking her.

'Well, I'll have plenty of time to get it shiny when you're off travelling round the globe.' Priti bit her tongue. 'I didn't mean that. I'm sorry.' She got up to give Jyoti a hug but her friend moved away to the window.

'It's OK, sweetie, but just remember it's not my fault you won't say no to your parents. And until you do, you're going to need that lamp. I hope it works for you. . .'

Priti picked up the tray and returned to the kitchen to refill the teapot and the plates of snacks. She had spent the morning cooking samosas and pakoras for the guests, who had clearly arrived this afternoon without bothering to eat any lunch. She refilled the plates and waited for the kettle to boil, pondering the best way to tackle the problem of RP. Yes, she knew the truth about him, but he was as wriggly as a worm, slippery, and just as slimy.

Pockets were not a feature of traditional clothes for women, but the skirt of Priti's pastel pink Indian suit had them. Fed up with the same old impractical designs, she had begun designing her own clothes, with her personal take on 'traditional', much to her mother's chagrin. 'But, Mummyji, it is the new fashion in Mumbai now. Everyone has dresses like this,' she would say, which lessened her mother's displeasure. There was nothing her mother wanted more than for Priti to be like all the other girls.

Deep in the right-hand pocket of her dress was Priti's miniature Aladdin's lamp.

She took it out and held it in the palm of her hand. It was really quite beautiful. She had soaked it in water overnight to make it easier to wash away the ingrained dirt, and cleaned it meticulously until it beamed with a warm lustre. It would never shine brilliantly like gold but it was more precious to her than all the gold in the world. It was Jyoti's parting gift, given with love. Priti clutched the lamp tightly to her heart, wishing with all her being that things were different, that the world was a kinder, more accepting and forgiving place. . .

No good asking for the moon. Be sensible in your wishes and do not waste them – you have but three. And, no, your third wish cannot be to ask for a thousand more wishes.

Startled, Priti spun round. She was alone in the kitchen, so where had the voice come from?

In the same weary, bored tone, the voice continued. *Come along now, do not be all day about it.*

Someone was playing a trick on her. 'Who are you? Where are you?' Priti searched the kitchen, half-expecting to find an old man lurking out of sight. 'Show yourself!' She stepped out of the back door into the courtyard, but it was empty. She returned to the kitchen. There was no one there. 'What are you?' she whispered, suddenly afraid.

I am the granter of wishes, and I am here, inside the lamp. Did you expect me to materialise in front of you? That requires the expenditure of rather a lot of unnecessary energy. Far better I reserve it for the tasks you wish of me.

Priti held the lamp aloft in her hand. *A genie?* Her fear gave way to a sense of awe, and excitement.

Come along, child, ask of me what you wish.

The voice was sounding irritated.

There were so many things that Priti could have wished for but the extraordinary situation she found herself in drove all logical thought from her mind. What should she wish for first? To be rid of all the suitors who came knocking? For Jyoti to never leave her? For her family to accept her for who she really was? For wealth and riches? For health? For happiness?

She had to think fast. She had to work out what was important to her. What were the three most important things? Ah, but would the genie, or whoever he was, really grant her all three wishes? She had read that some genies could be very tricky and that if you did not phrase your wish in precisely the correct manner, they might find a way to twist your words.

'First, before I wish for anything at all, tell me the rules. How many wishes do I really have? Are there tasks that are beyond your control, or things that I cannot wish for? Will you twist my words?'

I am affronted by your impertinence, child. Of course there is no trickery involved. Tell me your first wish and be done with it.

Now he sounded extremely angry. Priti delayed no longer. She asked to be granted her first wish.

'I wish . . . I wish that RP and his uncle would go away,' she said.

Your wish is my command.

'OK, so how does this work?'

There was no response.

'Hello?'

Nothing.

The genie had gone. Priti tucked the brass lamp back into her pocket, poured the water over the tea leaves in the pot and carried the tray back through to the living room. This time there was a tentative smile on her face.

RP was still holding court and her parents were still nodding their heads in agreement with everything he said. Priti wondered how the genie would tackle this particular task. He had his work cut out.

A loud ring cut short RP's monologue and he rummaged in his pockets for his phone. 'So sorry,' he muttered, frowning at the caller ID. 'I must take this.' His finger stabbed the phone to answer it as he scurried from the room.

Was the phone call the genie's doing? There was nothing for it but to wait and see.

Priti's parents made small talk with RP's uncle but his answers were as vague as his nephew's, and very quickly he steered the conversation back to the matter of the arrangements for the impending engagement

79

and wedding which, for someone from a small village, he seemed to know a great deal about. 'Visas and entry requirements must be met, you understand. The Americans are extremely strict about that kind of thing. But do not worry, I will handle all of those matters.'

Priti's heart was sinking. If the genie did not act soon, she would be engaged, married and bundled off to a strange country on an alien continent.

She would have to say something – at the very least it might alert her parents to RP's suspect character. They always said they had her best interests at heart, so she was sure they would want to investigate him further before tying her to him.

'I googled your nephew,' she began. 'Did you know that you can google anyone? It's possible to find out so much about a person these days.'

The uncle's smile wavered for a fraction of a second.

'For example, your nephew just tweeted, "India is full of naive young girls with parents happy to give them away to the highest bidder #landofmilkandhoney".'

'Priti, you are being ridiculous,' her mother chided. 'That was obviously not our RP.'

First her mum had started calling him *beta*, as though he was already part of the family, and now *our* RP? Since when had he become 'ours'?

RP rushed back into the room all in a fluster. 'I'm sorry, but I have been summoned back to the city for an urgent meeting. I must leave immediately. But do not fear, I promise to return as soon as I have dealt with this most unexpected and urgent matter. Please accept my deepest apologies,' he said, extending his hand to Priti's father. He clasped his hands together in front of Priti's mother. 'My apologies again. Come, Uncle, we must leave at once.'

Within a few minutes they were out of the house, bundled into their car and gone, leaving nothing but clouds of dry dust billowing in their wake.

Priti resisted the temptation to dance with joy until she was in her bedroom with the door firmly shut, and only then did she jump up and down in elation. She lay down on her bed and wondered at the strangeness of the day – the genie, the suitor, the suddenness of his departure, and RP's promise to return. Priti had a feeling she would never see RP again. Surely the phone call had been the genie's doing, or had it more simply been a matter of serendipity? Would she ever know, she wondered. And would RP ever make good on his promise and return? Time would tell.

But she had better make sure, she thought. She took the brass lamp out of her pocket and summoned the genie.

'I wish that all the suitors would go away and never come back,' she declared.

Very well, the genie answered. *Your wish is my command.*

Many years later. . .

Priti sat on the edge of her bed, the little brass lamp in her hands. She was in what had once been her parents' room. They had long since passed away, bequeathing the house to her. Priti had not asked for the house, not once in all the years she had stayed with them, caring for them as they had aged, sickened and then died, but she was grateful to them that they had given it to her, for where else would she go? Still, she wondered what to do with a house that was too big for one person. Her siblings urged her to sell it and to use the money to go abroad, to study, to travel, to find someone to settle down with. They were so anxious that she find a suitable man – it was not common for a woman to remain alone and unmarried, and for as long as she stayed in this state, she remained their responsibility.

No suitor had darkened her door for many years, and none would. The genie had made good on his promise. She summoned him for the third time now she was in her forties and asked him if it was his doing, and he muttered that he had only done as she had wished.

'By suitors I meant male suitors.'

You did not specify gender, the genie had replied irritably.

'Were there other suitors then, after RP?'

Several. One of them was most persistent.

Which one? But Priti did not utter those words aloud because she knew it would break her heart.

Tears welled in her eyes.

It would be better to let the pieces of her history lie in rest.

Downstairs, the sounds of children's laughter could be heard. She had opened her arms and filled her house with lost children, taken them into her heart and filled the lonely places. Yet one place remained untouched.

She heard her name being called from downstairs and hurried to answer. The brass lamp she threw into the bin on her way down.

Bina, one of the oldest girls in the house, rescued several years ago from the streets, entered Madam Priti's room to sweep the floor and make her bed. She did not mind this chore. Madam Priti's room was a haven of tranquillity, away from the hubbub twenty children created in the rest of the house. As she emptied the bin, she spotted an antique brass lamp, small enough to fit into her pocket. She settled it there, wondering why Madam Priti would throw away such a beautiful old lamp. When everyone had gone to bed that night, she would polish it until it shone again.

She was sure it would bring her luck.

Next Stop, the Eiffel Tower

by Miriam Halahmy

My laptop pings. It's Saskia on Skype.

'Hey, party girl. Finished packing?' Saskia blows me a kiss. 'Bring me back a hot French boy. You are so lucky. Three amazing days in Paris.'

'Isn't it awesome?' I say, picking up a strappy top and folding it for my case. 'Next stop, the Eiffel Tower.'

'WhatsApp me every twenty minutes. Wish my mum was a famous author. Bye, sweetie.' She blows me another kiss and logs off.

Mum's new book, *Looking for Farid*, just won the UK TeenLit Prize, which is impressive. So she's a bit famous now.

I give a little skip and open my underwear drawer. Mum's been invited to a Paris lycée to talk about her book and because it's half term I get my dream trip. We leave in the morning. I'm going to wear skinny jeans, my best top, Converse trainers and sunglasses.

'Madina Sinead Dolan, haven't you finished packing yet?' Mum's standing in my doorway, grinning, hair loose down her back. She's shorter than me now and she's kept her figure but a couple of lines have appeared on her forehead. She hates them. We have the same dark hair but mine's curly like Dad's and I spend ages with straightners.

'Only one suitcase?' says Mum.

'I bet you're taking the big one,' I mutter, as I wrestle with the zip on my make-up bag.

She flicks her hair back and says, 'I'm setting the alarm for five. . .'

'What?'

'The train leaves at seven. We have to be in Paris at midday and at the lycée for two. Peace can't wait,' and she goes off to her room, ignoring my groan.

The lycée's doing a peace project and Mum's book is about human rights and asylum seekers. I get a lot of peace stuff around the dinner table. Mostly I switch off because there's only so much thinking one girl can do. I want to be a fashion journalist and travel round the world interviewing models.

Mum's from a Lebanese Muslim family and Dad's Irish Catholic from Belfast, 'So, Yasmin Dolan,' Dad loves saying to Mum, 'we're a proper little peace project all by ourselves, isn't that the truth?' We're not a religious family, no hijabs or Hail Marys. But Mum thinks I'm going to 'learn a lot' on this trip, so I've been very, very careful not to mention hot French boys or even the Eiffel Tower.

The Eurostar journey's not as much fun as I thought it would be and by the time we arrive at the Gare du Nord I'm starving.

'Come on, *habibti*,' Mum says as she strides off.

'Can't we just grab a snack?' I call after her as she cuts through a line of tourists. I spot some police in military style uniforms with guns at their hips. One of them has an Alsatian on a short chain. I give them a wide berth and look round. Where's Mum? What if I'm lost or she's lost or been arrested at gunpoint for writing subversive books?

'Madinaaaahh!'

I spin round and Mum's standing at the top of a flight of steps. I yank my case forward but a woman pushing a buggy screams at me. I swerve and trip over. My case rips out of my hand and spins across the station floor. There's an outburst from the police and the dog snarls. God!

A policeman grabs the case and I go and take it from him, muttering, *'Merci, monsieur.'* He glares at me.

So this is Paris; crowded, noisy and armed to the teeth. For a minute I wish I was back home, giggling with Saskia over some stupid vid on YouTube.

'For goodness sakes, Madina,' Mum snaps as I finally reach her. 'Keep up. We have to find the right metro.' We lug our bags down flights and flights of stairs. Haven't they heard of escalators here? Eventually we throw ourselves onto a train and collapse on a couple of very hard seats.

'We're going to Porte d'Orleans,' Mum mumbles as she checks her map. She looks all hot and bothered. 'Maryam Hussein, the English teacher, will meet us there. Our hotel's nearby – I hope it's clean.'

The train sets off and I call out the station names. 'Saint Michel. . .'

'No, in French you pronounce it "san".'

'Vavinne . . . or is it "van". . .?' I throw her a glance. She has her worried look on. Mum always gets worked up before a school visit.

But she smiles and says, 'You'll pick up loads of vocab this trip, won't you?'

She sounds like a teacher but I'm trying to keep on her right side so I say, *'Alesseea.'* I know it's wrong but she'll enjoy putting me right, which she does, and then it's our stop and we jump off, up yet another two flights of stairs and finally into the fresh air. Hallelujah!

We're right outside a shop which says, *Boulangerie.* 'Hold my case,' I snap at Mum and before she can stop me, I've dived in the shop and come out with a long baguette.

Mum's standing with a woman. I'm already stuffing warm crunchy bread in my mouth. 'Maryam,' says Mum with a frown at me, 'this is my daughter, Madina.'

Maryam's taller than Mum, with the same olive-brown skin and dark hair. She's wearing a brown scarf round her neck, grey top and brown trousers. 'Hello, Madina,' she says and gives me a warm smile. 'Welcome to Paris.'

'Thank you,' I say.

'Now we will go to your hotel and then we will have lunch,' says Maryam. 'You must be very hungry.'

The hotel's OK and we have lunch in a nearby cafe. Then we walk to the lycée. I managed to change into a clean top in my room and touched up my make-up, and now as we get near, I can see some older boys ahead of us. They don't wear uniform in Paris – heavenly – so the students are wearing all kinds of stuff. The girls are a mixture of skinny jeans like me and sort-of dark trousers and long tops. No one wears the hijab. Maybe they don't have Muslims in French schools.

We're swept along corridors and upstairs into a large room with a big circle of chairs in the middle. Students are coming through the door in twos and threes, tapping on phones and dropping onto chairs. It feels so, well, grown up.

I look around and a boy with shoulder-length light-brown hair parted in the middle and wearing a worn jean jacket waves to me. He's sitting in a group of boys and girls.

'Hello,' says the boy with a smile as I go over. He has a heavy accent. 'I am Jean Luc. And I think you are coming to see us from London?'

I smile back and sit down, relieved someone is talking to me. 'Yes, that's right. I'm Madi. That's my mum, Yasmin Dolan.' I nod towards Mum who's shuffling through papers and glancing nervously round the room. I catch her eye and give her the thumbs up.

'*C'est* cool,' says a girl behind me.

Well, that's new vocab then, isn't it?

Maryam steps forward and introduces Mum. I think they've all read her book, *Looking for Farid*. It's about two boys from Syria: Farid, sixteen and Nabil, thirteen. Their parents are killed and they run away to Greece. Farid finds a place for them on a lorry to England. It's dark and crowded in the lorry and the brothers are separated. When they arrive at Dover, Farid is not there. Poor Nabil is taken to a children's home and the rest of the book is the search for Farid with a very bittersweet ending. It really deserved the prize.

Mum opens with a short reading from the book. Then she talks about attitudes towards asylum seekers in France and the UK, how political groups campaign against immigration and how this fuels racism and even more conflict and war. She quotes a bit of graffiti you see around London – 'You cannot fight for peace, you have to peace for peace.'

'It seems to me,' she says, 'that we have to do a lot of listening if we really believe in peace and tolerance. We have to listen to the other's point of view even if that is really hard to hear. A student in England once told me that his father says all Muslims support terrorism.'

I remember that. I was so shocked when she told us at dinner that night and Dad shook his head as if he'd heard it all before.

'I'm not religious,' Mum's saying, 'although I come from a Lebanese Muslim family. But I listened to the student. If I'd just shouted or walked away nothing would have changed. We had a good discussion and he said he would speak to his father.'

A girl says, 'No one listens in France. Why we should even try?'

'We must try for peace,' says someone else.

'Why listen? No one listen to me because I am Muslim. The *gouvernement* hate Muslim. We cannot wear the hijab to school so I hate them!' another girl yells out.

Suddenly I realise that Maryam should be wearing that scarf over her hair and not round her neck and there are girls in the class who could be Muslim but no one has covered their hair.

Maryam nods and says, 'In French schools we are not allowed to wear any religious symbols, no hijabs, crosses or kippahs. But that doesn't mean that we cannot be proud to be Christians, Muslims or Jews in France.'

So that's why the Muslim girls don't have their hair covered. The Muslim girls at my school wouldn't like that and they don't seem to here either. It definitely feels weird.

'*Non, Madame,*' says a small voice behind me. I look round and it's a girl with pale skin and very large dark eyes. Maryam nods to encourage her. The girl says, 'I cannot say out loud in France today that I am proud to be Jewish.'

'Why not?' I blurt out, amazed.

Everyone cranes round to look at me and I feel a right idiot.

'It is not safe,' says the girl. 'Jewish men take off their kippahs after synagogue – my father and my brother do not wear them outside or they might be attacked.'

'But in London you see kippahs all the time,' I say, looking at Mum, who nods back.

'There is much work to do on peace and tolerance,' says Maryam, 'and our discussions with Yasmin will be very helpful.'

There's a snort from across the circle. It's the girl who hates the government. She mutters something in French and a couple of people snigger.

Jean Luc whispers to me, 'She is Dina. She hate everyone.' He grins and I grin back, staring into his eyes which are a really light grey. My heart flutters and all I can think is, *I need to WhatsApp Saskia. I think I'm totally falling in love.*

The rest of the session flies by and then the school day is over.

What now? I think, hanging back as Mum chats to Maryam and everyone starts leaving with their friends.

Then Jean Luc comes over and says, 'Go with us to have coffee.'

An electric thrill goes through me and I turn to Mum who's eyeing Jean Luc.

'Please, Mum,' I say. I feel like a little kid who's been asked round for a play date.

'Hmm, well,' says Mum. 'Jean Luc you must stay with Madina all the time and bring her back for seven to our hotel. Do you understand?' She has a deep frown on her face, which means, Don't mess with me.

Jean Luc nods and says, 'I promise, *Madame*, I will bring her to you very safe.'

Mum hesitates as I hold my breath and then she says, 'OK,' and as she calls out all sorts of instructions after me, we dash out of the room, downstairs and into Paris!

I feel like I've been released from a huge cage and now here I am in a foreign city, hundreds of miles from home and absolutely anything could happen.

As we walk away from the school, Jean Luc and his friends fool about, laughing and putting earphones into each other's ears to listen to music, just like me and Sask do. The streets are quite narrow with lots of small shops and I can smell fresh bread again, and coffee coming out of one of the cafes. A scooter whizzes past with two boys not wearing helmets and Jean Luc shouts out to them. They wave back, swerving round a car that has stopped in the middle of the road. The driver yells out of his window and Jean Luc says with a grin, 'Bad words, I don't translate to you.'

'No worries,' I say and I wonder if he knows I'm only fifteen. Jean Luc and his friends must be at least seventeen – they're all in *Les Terminals,* which is like our Upper Sixth. Sask will be so impressed.

We turn a corner into an alleyway and then Jean Luc says, 'It is here.'

The cafe's called La Palette. Inside there's a couple of old blokes leaning on the bar and a few tables and chairs. No one's drinking coffee.

Jean Luc takes my hand and a glow goes through me as he leads me to a door at the back of the cafe. We go down a steep flight of stairs to a basement where someone's playing a guitar. It's quite dim at the bottom but there are candles glowing in corners and then I see a short, thin boy sitting on a wooden box, slapping it in time to the music. There are big cushions on the floor and Jean Luc pulls me down. The others settle around us and start nodding in time to the music. It's quite hypnotic. Jean Luc puts his arm around me and I snuggle up. My heart's thumping like a slapped wooden crate.

I can hear Saskia's voice in my ear, 'Whoo hoo, send details.'

'*Un demi?*' says Max, a boy with a blond ponytail. He's offering me a glass of beer, about a half pint. Everyone seems to be drinking and I remember I have mints in my bag so Mum won't guess.

'*Merci,*' I say and then I raise the glass and call out, 'Cheers.'

They all call 'cheers' back.

'We teach you French words and you teach us English, *d'accord*, OK?' says Simone, the Jewish girl from class. Her face is more relaxed now and she seems quite friendly.

'*Oui, d'accord,*' I say and pulling my phone out I say, 'Selfie?'

Max immediately drops down in front of us, laughing and pushing Jean Luc who gives him a friendly punch. But then Simone leans her cheek against Jean Luc's shoulder. Are they an item, I wonder, and a pang of jealousy goes through me.

Jean Luc grabs the phone and takes the picture, his long arm stretching out in front of us.

I check it and it seems full of Simone's big dark eyes. I'm just thinking of suggesting another photo when Max takes out what is definitely a spliff and lights it. He takes a drag and offers it to me. Oh God! If Mum smells that on me I'll be grounded for life. I shake my head and Simone exchanges a look with Jean Luc. The beer's already going to my head and I feel myself going hot and red.

Time to go? But then Simone peels away and wanders off to the guitar player who's absolutely gorgeous. He has a chiselled jaw, white-blond hair and tattoos all up his arms. He looks too old for school.

Jean Luc murmurs in my ear, 'You enjoy Paris, Madi?'

'Yeah, great,' I say.

'Do you want to visit any place here?'

'The Eiffel Tower, but Mum doesn't think we'll have time.'

'I take you tomorrow morning.'

'We have class, don't we?'

'Do we?'

'Well. . .'

'Meet me at Porte d'Orleans at eight.'

His grey eyes are twinkling and I feel myself melt. The music's stopped and Simone's sitting on the knee of the gorgeous guitarist. So that's OK, then.

'Skip class?' I say with a mock disapproving look and he shrugs back with a grin.

I'll make sure Mum doesn't even know and to be honest, I've had enough of peace and tolerance for a bit.

Jean Luc leans over and kisses me on the lips. It's like I've died and gone to heaven.

Oh. My. God. He IS hot.

Isn't he. . .? We're bunking off tomoz going to Eiffel T

Awesome. Sooo jealous. Do you have one for me?

I'm lying in bed WhatsApping with Sask. I send her a pic of the guitarist.

I think he's taken but you could give it a go

She sends me back about ten Emojis.

I'm too excited to sleep. Mum hasn't guessed anything. She's worried about the workshop tomorrow.

I finally drop off and then Mum's knocking on my door.

'Coming,' I moan in a weak voice.

'Breakfast in ten minutes, Madina, and then we have to walk to school. They start at eight here.'

'Don't feel well,' I call back.

'What? Open the door.'

I get up and let her in and then I crawl back under the covers.

'What's the matter, *habibti*?'

'I've got a really bad headache and I feel sick.'

She stares at me for a moment and then she says, 'OK, stay here this morning. I'll come back at lunchtime and you can join us this afternoon.'

Result! 'Thanks, Mum.'

I close my eyes and roll over as she goes out. Then I jump out of bed and start getting ready. Mum calls out to me again as she leaves for school and then I'm all alone and free. Jean Luc! The Eiffel Tower!

I skip downstairs and out of the door into a cloudy Paris morning. Cars are honking and people are hurrying to work. Some men are standing at a counter in the cafe next door, sipping tiny cups of black coffee. There's a pile of croissants in a bakery window and I go in and buy one. It's so buttery and flaky I polish it off in seconds. Then I look up and down the street. Which way to the metro?

There's a woman coming towards me in a slick office suit, heels tapping on the pavement and I say, '*Excusez-moi Madame, ou se trouve le metro?*'

She waves her hand over her shoulder and lets out a stream of instructions. But I get the general idea. I thank her and soon I'm crossing over the Boulevard Péripherique which roars round Paris like a crazy motorway. I glance at my watch. Jean Luc should be there by now.

The streets get even busier near the metro. I pass a man talking loudly into his phone. He has a black bag over his shoulder like a camera bag. Maybe he's a photographer. My mind wanders off into a daydream about being a fashion journalist. My English teacher's going to get me work experience on a magazine. Mum thinks I write with real flare so—

My thoughts are cut off by what sounds like a car backfiring, and then again and again. A woman lets out a blood-curdling scream, waving her arms about, eyes wide with fear. I turn my head and see the man with the camera case fall but it's like slow motion, his legs crumpling bit by bit, very slowly. The scream fills every corner of my head until the man is on the ground and dark red liquid pours onto the pavement from under his back.

Cars skid to a halt and people throw themselves onto the ground and through shop doorways. I clutch my bag to my body and dive behind a car as there are more sharp cracks. It's gunfire. I'm going to be killed. I'm only fifteen. I'm too young to die. I huddle down, shaking and crying, making myself as small as possible. Then I hear footsteps pound towards me and as I raise my eyes in terror I see two men, faces covered with black masks, racing along, huge machine guns in their hands.

They'll kill me, I think, but I can't look away and for a split second I meet the eyes of one of the men. It's as though I'm mesmerised. He has one green eye and one blue eye. So weird. Then he's gone and all I want to do is roll under the wheels of the car and stay there forever.

But an arm is pulling me up and a voice is speaking in French. I stare up into the face of a policeman in his dark-blue military uniform. He pulls me to my feet and I lean against his chest, sobbing and sobbing.

Sirens are wailing, people shout and moan, and above all the noise a voice screams out, 'Madi!'

It's Jean Luc and he's speaking to the policeman, saying *'Anglais'*, over and over.

All I can think is, *I want my Mum.*

'You're an important witness, Madi darling, and the police need to speak to you tomorrow after they've done some more investigations, sure they do.'

It's evening and we're back in the hotel. This has been the worst day of my life. The police took me and Jean Luc to school to collect Mum. Her face when she knew what had happened was so awful I swear I will never ever do anything to upset her again. We had to go to the police station and give a statement for hours.

I want to go home but Dad's telling me I have to stay and so's Mum. I know they're right but I'm still shaking.

'Why did they do it, Dad, why?'

But I know. The dead man was a newspaper editor who published cartoons of the Prophet Mohammed. That's forbidden in Islam and many religious Muslims were insulted. So Islamic terrorists targeted him and killed him before the police arrived. One of the gunmen was killed but the other one escaped. The one with the different-coloured eyes. The one I saw.

'Ah, Madi, what can I tell you? You know when I was a kid in the Troubles in Belfast, your grandpa's surgery was bombed out twice on the Falls Road. It was like living on the front line in a war. But by helping the police you're doing your bit for peace like your mum does. What do you say, Madi?'

I'm silent for a bit and then I say, 'I suppose so.'

'That's my girl. I'll be waiting for you both at St Pancras tomorrow evening and we'll take a taxi home like royalty, so we shall.'

When we go out of the hotel the next morning there's a crowd of students from the lycée. I look round bewildered and see Simone and Max. They grin and then I spot Jean Luc standing to one side, just staring at me.

Max rolls up his sleeve and flexes his biceps. He looks such a clown I can't help smiling. 'We are walking with you,' he says, 'to . . . to—'

'Terrify the bad men,' cuts in Simone.

'Max could not scare a baby!' calls out one of the boys and everyone laughs.

'*C'est cool. Merci,*' I say in a small voice.

There are some whoops and Jean Luc comes over to me. When we set off, Mum and Simone walking together, Jean Luc puts his arm round me.

He checks that Mum is out of hearing and then he says, 'I am so, so sorry, Madi. *Je suis desolé . . . desolé. . .*'

'It wasn't your fault.'

'*Bof,* I should have come to the hotel and walked with you and, and . . . I am so sorry.'

He stares at me with such sad eyes. There's nothing much I can say, is there? I feel just as awful.

I could hardly sleep last night. I spoke to Sask on Mum's phone for an hour before I went to bed. I miss her so much.

Saskia WhatsApped this morning.

Tezza says he's gonna buy a gun and teach dem gangstas respect.
There were a dozen Emojis.

Mel G, Mel C, mad Bobby and even Miss Hammond send love. God, Mads what are you like? Wait till I get you home, my girl. You are so grounded!!

That made me smile a little bit. Miss Hammond's the English teacher who thinks I could be a journalist. Not sure I want to after all this.

We arrive at the lycée and go upstairs to the classroom. The room's quite noisy. Everyone's hyped up and a boy called Claude is arguing with Max in French. Max looks furious but then Maryam quietens everyone down.

We're all sitting in a circle when Claude suddenly stands up and points his finger at Maryam. 'You!' he says. Then he points at Mum and then at me!

'You and you,' he says. 'You are burning the French flag and killing people.'

There's uproar in the class. People are almost screaming, Mum's face looks drained and Maryam is waving her arms and calling for quiet.

I yell in Jean Luc's ear, 'What does he mean?'

Jean Luc shakes his head and says, 'Claude hate Muslim. He want them all out of France.'

'That's racist.'

'*Exactement.*'

The class eventually quietens down and Maryam puts the word 'You' on the board. Then she says, 'Those are very strong feelings, Claude, and as Yasmin said yesterday we should listen to each other. So now I ask you to listen. What do you mean by "You"? I am French, like you, and so are all the other Muslim students in the lycée.'

Claude lets out a stream of French and even I can work out the words are not polite. He kicks back his chair, which falls over with a crash, and strides out of the room.

I try to catch Mum's eye. I think we should leave. I have to see the police in an hour. Anyhow this is nothing to do with us, we're English.

But then Maryam looks at her watch and says quietly, 'It is time.'

Time for what?

Maryam says, 'We agreed yesterday to have a one-minute's silence for Arnaud Clement, the editor who was murdered yesterday.'

So we can't leave just yet. I lower my eyes like everyone else and there is silence.

But after only about ten seconds a chair scrapes back and a voice cries out, '*Non, Madame*. I cannot do this. I do not agree with this. . .' It is Dina, the girl who hates the government.

Max shouts at her, '*Ta gueule, Dina.*'

'*Ta gueule, toi!*' Dina snaps back.

I think that means, *Shut your mouth.*

'Dina, what is this now?' says Maryam in a tired voice.

'Every day hundreds of people die in Syria!' Dina is shouting. 'We never have a minute's silence for them because they are Muslim and in France no one care about Muslim. . .'

She's ranting on and on and Mum's dropped her head and she looks so worn out. The attack yesterday seems to have taken all the spark out of her. I have to do something to make her feel better.

I jump up and call out, 'You don't care about anything, let alone peace!'

Dina stops midstream and a rumble goes round the room. Suddenly I think of Dad's voice saying, 'Like living on the front line.'

That's it, isn't it? Who knows where the next attack will be? A holiday beach, a mosque, a supermarket? Malala got shot just because she went to school.

'Dina,' I say, looking straight at her and she frowns, seemingly surprised I know her name. 'If you're really upset about Syria, then do something. Join a peace organisation or . . . or . . . make a video about our work this week and put it up on YouTube. Make people listen to you. If you just complain, you're making war not peace. We're all living on the front line now. No one can ignore what's going on in the world. We're all responsible.'

'*Bravo, Madi!*' It's Simone and she's standing too. 'I hate what happen here in Paris and it is not the first time. But now I make my mind up. I am going to raise my voice for peace everyday from now on.'

Whistles and cheers flood the room and Mum's standing up, her head raised, smiling at me. That's enough peace for me.

We arrive back at the Gare du Nord to catch our Eurostar train to London and I can't wait to see Dad and Saskia and everyone else. The police think they know who the other terrorist is and they'll hunt him down quite soon. All I want is to go home.

But then above the noise of the crowds I hear voices calling, 'Madi, hey, Madi!'

I turn and there's Simone waving and calling out. Max is with her, blowing hard into some huge rubber thing in his arms. Jean Luc runs up behind them and when they reach me Max stops blowing, pushes in the plug and hands me a gigantic model of the Eiffel Tower.

I give a scream and say, 'Awesome! I love it!'

'Don't forget us,' says Simone and she kisses me on both cheeks the French way. Max does the same and then Jean Luc elbows him out of the way.

'We . . . I will miss you, Madi. You are a special person. I am sorry about. . .' He falters and Mum pats him on the arm. 'But when I come to London you can show me your tower.'

His grey eyes crinkle in a grin as I give him a puzzled look.

'Tower of London,' says Mum, tutting and raising her eyes.

She moves off with Simone and Max to look at a souvenir shop.

I fiddle with the buttons on my jacket and it seems an age as I stand there with Jean Luc staring at the floor. Then he takes me in his arms and I'm about to say, *'Au revoir'*, when he kisses me on the lips – a proper, grown-up-boyfriend kiss.

Wait till I tell Saskia!

The Day I Told the Truth

by Keren David

Mom was smoking dope in the living room and Dad was doing t'ai chi in the kitchen. Upstairs, I was breaking up with Tim because he was stupid enough to have fallen in love with me.

Welcome to my world of dysfunction.

Eighty per cent of the time my mom is not a dopehead. That's because eighty per cent of the time she's not here, she's in some war zone or wherever, helping refugees. That's not just her job, it's her passion, it's her reason for living, it's everything.

'What you don't realise, Ethan, is how rewarding it is when your job matters more than anything else,' she'd told me last time we'd discussed my total inability to achieve anything that she thinks is worthwhile, a topic that comes up a lot when she bothers to come home.

'Yeah, right, thanks, I get it,' I'd replied, my usual response when she starts preaching the path of righteousness. 'Why don't you piss off back to Afghanistan and leave me in peace?'

Then she started sighing and telling me that I shouldn't be hostile because we have so little precious time together, and when she's home in Amsterdam it's important to be calm and peaceful, 'Because this is my oasis, Ethan darling, my place to revive body and spirit, to fill up my energy stores before I go out into the field again. You'll understand one day when you find your vocation.' Then she went into her bedroom and lit up a joint, and I found her an ashtray and opened a window because I hate the smell of the stuff, and I'd just finished her room – the paint was still tacky and I didn't want any ash sticking to it.

Anyway, she'd been smoking more than usual since Dad arrived in Amsterdam. No one invited him. He just decided for the first time that I couldn't possibly be left alone in the house when Mom went away, so he was going to come and live with me for six months (at least – Mom's assignments generally overrun by at least fifty per cent).

'I'm seventeen,' I pointed out when he arrived. 'If you didn't bother when I was fourteen, why are you here now?'

'I did bother. You used to come and stay with me for all your holidays.'

'Yeah, but you never came here and moved in on me.'

'That's because I had Sandra and the boys to think of.'

'Oh well, lucky me that you dumped them.' Sandra was OK as stepmothers go – she didn't actively loathe me and her kids were a lot younger than me, but they were positively friendly. They made holidays with Dad infinitely easier because I didn't have to talk to him very much.

'I didn't dump them. Sandra and I decided . . . mutually decided. . .'

'Yeah, whatever.'

I had no interest. He clearly wanted somewhere to stay rent-free now his marriage had broken down. Dad has his own vocation which is creative writing, but it doesn't seem to involve actually making any cash. He loves nurturing, mentoring, helping people find their way. I keep on trying to tell him that I'm not on a creative journey, I'm not going anywhere, just because I like making films and pictures and stuff, but he will not listen.

Anyway, this was Mom's last assignment before I turned eighteen and became an adult, and Dad was making a huge deal of it. I'd have been quite happy on my own. Mom's friend Mieke used to move in to look after me when Mom was away, and she'd have kept an eye on me this time. Not that I needed her. I'm not a kid any more. In fact, I never really felt like a kid at all.

So, Mum was smoking dope, Dad was doing t'ai chi and I was breaking up with Tim. Pretty, stupid Tim – Tim who'd been hanging around in my room for a couple of hours seriously doing my head in, because I can't really tolerate company for more than forty-five minutes or so, and my room is my space. I'll make an exception if we're actually having sex, OK, but we'd finished that and I just wanted him to leave.

We'd been seeing each other for about a month after a random encounter at the Pride parade. Normally I give it a miss but our friend Bart was on one of the boats and Rosa insisted that we go along to support him. And it was kind of funny seeing string-bean Bart dressed as a sailor, his many pimples coated with his mom's foundation, gyrating to Justin Bieber and waving madly when he spotted us.

Rosa and I had got there early. We found a place to sit on the Prinsengracht, legs dangling over the canal-side, and she was loving the music and waving to people, but once Bart had gone past, I got bored and realised how much I hated crowds and noise and all that crap – all the happiness. So I decided to go home.

Rosa shook her head when I told her, but she couldn't be bothered to argue because she knew there was no point. Rosa knows me inside out, which is why she's my best friend. (I only have about ten friends so there's not a lot of competition for the job.)

Anyway, as I pushed my way through the people, I stumbled and bumped into this guy – this amazing-looking guy. Huge brown eyes, like a cow's. Soft blonde hair, like a horse's mane (not a real horse – a kind of fantasy Pegasus horse). Shoulders like Thor. Hands like a pianist. Despite myself – I never do this – I smiled. He smiled back. We walked down the Utrechtestraat together, swapping stories. He was American, in Amsterdam for a year on an international student exchange thing. I made high-school dropout sound more interesting than it is. And when we reached the little park on the Frederiksplein we stopped to kiss. Easy. Simple. Just as I like it.

And just a few weeks later, here we were breaking up, as inevitable as my mom getting all excited when there's a natural disaster or a civil war.

Tim started it. 'I want us to be together. Properly. You know. Boyfriends. I think I love you.'

In one fluid movement I was out of bed and across to the window. 'The rain's stopped,' I told him. 'Sorry to kick you out but I've got something I have to do. I can't lie in bed all day.'

He blinked at me. Anyone with a heart would have melted, he was so adorable-looking. Kitten-in-a-basket cute.

Luckily – and I have it on good authority – I have no heart.

'Ethan, I'm sorry. I said the wrong thing.'

'That's OK.' I could hear my voice sounded clipped and curt, cold as a winter night on a North Sea beach. 'I just don't do that whole relationship thing.'

He grinned. 'But we're so good together. Won't you just think about it?'

No, I thought. *No. Nee. Never.*

'I'm sorry,' I lied. 'I think you'd better go.'

'I don't mind, honestly.'

'Mind what?'

'That you're . . . you know. . .'

I knew.

'Well, thank you for your tolerance,' I drawled. 'Look, you'd better just leave now.' I nodded towards the door. 'Go that way so my parents don't see you.'

His eyes widened. 'They don't know?'

'They don't know what?'

'About you.'

I laughed, because it seemed the most appropriate response. 'They don't know the first thing about me, no.'

'But you should tell them.'

'What, some great coming-out ceremony? I don't think so.'

'Ethan, you know I can support you through this. It's important. They're your parents. You can't live your life in the closet.'

I didn't say anything. I just nodded towards the door, and eventually – five painful, silent minutes later – he left. And I breathed in and out and told myself that I didn't care, that he hadn't said anything, that I could just ignore him.

I was not in the closet. My friends knew (all ten of them). In fact I'd slept with most of them.

And as far as my parents were concerned, there wasn't even a closet to be in because they mostly lived elsewhere. My furniture wasn't in their homes. So they weren't exactly sitting, waiting for me to come out of it. They just had no idea at all who I was and why I did anything.

And that was just fine with me, because I like to be private.

Except. Rosa thought I should tell them. And Mieke did as well. And they are the two people I care about the most since my Grandpa Sam died.

Rosa had started on at me as soon as she'd heard Dad was coming over. We were in the Vondelpark, that quiet bit past the rose garden, lying on a blanket, staring at the grass.

'What are you scared of?' she said. 'They're going to be fine about it. They'll be happy you told them. It'll be special.'

'Speak *Nederlands*,' I told her. 'I'm not a kid any more. I can cope.'

She wriggled closer. I could smell that Rosa scent, patchouli and peaches and lilac.

'You know I love to speak English. Why have you gone all tense?' She started kneading my shoulders through my T-shirt.

I do know she loves to speak English. Her love of English was fed by Harry Potter films and a dad who belongs to a society where Dutch people – I kid you not – read Charles Dickens aloud. It saved my sorry ass when I started school in Amsterdam. The other kids could all speak

English but they thought it was funny to watch me flounder. Rosa saved me a million times.

'I'm not tense,' I said, rolling over onto my back so she couldn't rub it any more. She wasn't put off. She just manoeuvred herself so she was lying half on top of me, cuddling me close. And it was very nice, so I just closed my eyes again and tried not to listen to her.

'You'll feel so much happier. Just tell them the truth.'

'I can't anyway,' I said. 'They're never together. Dad lives in England. Mom is a world citizen.' *And they hate each other's guts,* I added silently.

'Excuses, Ethan. There's such a thing as Skype.'

I'd tried to imagine it. Setting up a three-way Skype. Mum actually making it, not being called away on some emergency.

Saying, 'I've got something to tell you.' Having their attention.

'You have no idea,' I told her. Then I grabbed her round the waist and rolled over so I was on top of her and I could duck my head down and lose myself in kissing her. Rosa was the first person I ever slept with and we come back to each other every time.

But she's seeing some guy from the university, some chunky hockey jock, so after a few kisses she pulled away and said, 'Got to go, *schaatje.* I've got an assignment to work on.' And she got up on her bike and rolled away, leaving me pissed off, frustrated and a little bit sad.

But anyway. Mum was in the bedroom smoking dope. Dad was doing t'ai chi in the kitchen. And Tim was gone. And I was still feeling that lingering sadness, although I didn't really know why.

Maybe I should do it, I thought. *Maybe there is a point. Maybe if I can trust them we can all get over the thing – the thing we never talk about. The day I told the truth.*

I waited until the night before Mom was leaving. Normally, she and I go out on her last evening. There's an Indonesian place we like where she can get vegetarian food, and she tells me all about where she's going and who's fighting who, and how many refugees there are, and what she hopes to do for them.

Of course, when I was really little she used to take me along with her, so I could experience first-hand the life of a refugee or whatever. She thought it'd help me grow up into someone who wanted to save the world, who realised that most problems aren't actually that serious by comparison. She ended up with a kid who wet the bed and had screaming nightmares, a broken marriage and a massive custody battle.

The nightmares calmed down eventually, but the bed-wetting went on and on. It wasn't a great way to establish a relationship with a stepmother, put it that way, although Sandra tried hard to be incredibly nice about it.

I do realise, though, then and now, that my problems are miniscule and unimportant, as is my life generally, so that was worthwhile.

Anyway, it all worked out because there we were, sitting around the table, Mom, Dad and me, quite the nuclear family. They agreed to share a vegetarian *rijstafel*. I ordered *ayam goreng* and yellow rice. Mum wrinkled her nose but she didn't say anything. I suppose she couldn't be bothered to have the conversation yet again when she tells me how they slaughter chickens and how frying them clogs your arteries.

'So, how long are you actually staying for?' I asked Dad, because it was probably good to get his answer in front of a witness.

'Well, certainly for the time Melinda is away,' he said, sprinkling coconut onto his plate. 'After she comes back, then we'll see. I have no special plans to go back to London. I'll have to look around for my own place.'

'I'm not being funny, but are you actually paying Mom rent? Because as I'm sort of looking after the house, maybe it should be paid straight to me?'

This is my vision for the future. Basically, Mom has no interest in Amsterdam apart from the fact that I needed somewhere to stay and go to school, etc, and she didn't want to be in London for obvious Dad reasons. And she likes the easy access to dope. But I'm not expecting she'll be around much once I turn eighteen. So, my argument is, let me rent out rooms on Airbnb, keep the place clean and nice, maybe offer breakfast for an extra charge. It'll be an income to fund my lifestyle of making art and rollerblading and listening to music and cooking. What's wrong with that?

But whenever I've tried to bring it up they both start banging on about college and qualifications and jobs and all that crap. As if they'd coordinated their response. As if they'd actually talked about it. It's very annoying.

OK, it is Mom's house, but she's made a will leaving it to me so there's a potential upside to her going off to war zones the whole time. That sounds callous, I know (Mieke told me). But when your parent is addicted to dangerous places, it's best to be realistic.

Dad gulped a bit. 'I could pay rent,' he said. 'Melinda?'

Mum assumed her most saintly expression. That's how she is around Dad now. All those battles over where I lived and where I went to school and who looked after me, all gone, forgotten, buried, paved over, without even a stone marking the spot. Now they are nice to each other, in a bland, false, syrupy way that makes me want to hide in a dark corner.

'That won't be necessary, Paul. You'll pay your way and look after Ethan, and that's a wonderful thing. You two need to build your relationship.'

I almost choked on my chicken.

'That's not what you said when you were trying to ban him from seeing me.'

'Time moves on. We heal and grow. You are becoming a man, Ethan. It will be helpful for you to spend time with Paul. You can learn from his mistakes, consider what path you want to take.'

Dad's mouth opened and closed. He looked intently at the dishes lined up on the burner in front of him. 'What's this one?' he asked.

'Fermented tempeh,' said Mom, smiling at him.

'I know what path I want to take,' I said, but all that achieved was an immediate closing of parental ranks. I should have realised years earlier that the way to bring them together was to refuse to take part in the whole school thing. All those years feeling miserable in classrooms in London, Amsterdam, Islamabad, Lagos.

As soon as I got that school wasn't actually compulsory, that I could just walk out, they started getting on. I was thirteen. I was stupid not to have done it before.

Now I ate my chicken and rice and rejected their ideas. Art college in London, Amsterdam, New York, no. Architecture – I'd love to be an architect, but I'd never survive the training – no thank you. Film school – forget it. Culinary college got a raised eyebrow. Working with orphans in Africa – I didn't even bother to respond.

Eventually they gave up. Dad put the college brochures back in his manbag. Mom said, 'I'm not agreeing to the Airbnb idea, Ethan, however much you sulk. I'm not having you live a parasitical existence.'

'What are you *talking* about?'

'You need to learn about good, honest labour. Even if you can't bring yourself to help other people, there's nothing wrong with you getting a job in a café, or a shop, or even cleaning. . .'

Huge eye-roll moment. 'Mom, those are all things I'd be doing if you'd just let me rent out rooms. But making reasonable money out of it, not just some pittance plus tips.'

'I see we've raised a capitalist,' said Dad and the two of them shared a merry little laugh that made me want to pick up my bowl of yellow rice and throw it at them.

But no. I don't do tantrums. Never have. I used to see other kids doing it, exploding with emotions, tears and snot and all the noise, and I'd sneer internally and despise them for their lack of control. At two years old, I swear it's true, I remember watching some boy called Robin lose control of his bladder at preschool in a furious storm over a toy car, and feeling coldly superior and very, very irritated. Now I'm seventeen anyway – way beyond the age of noise and stamping feet.

'Yeah, right, very funny,' I said. 'I'm happy you agree about something at last, even if it's only that what I want is ridiculous.'

'You know we care about what you want,' said Mom.

'No, I don't know that, actually,' I replied, although actually yes, I do know. They cared far too much about what I wanted at exactly the wrong time.

'Oh, Ethan. You do.'

'I know you think you care.'

Mom looked at me. She's beautiful, my mother. 'The angel of the refugee camps', according to some magazine, although Mieke tutted when she showed me the article, pointing out that it was both racist and sexist to make a big fuss of a woman just doing her job simply because she happens to be blonde and a former Miss East Texas 1995.

Mieke would never have gone in for a beauty contest, she doesn't make a fuss about anything and she only ever leaves Amsterdam once a year for two weeks in France. She's grouchy and always speaks her mind, and she and Rosa are the only people who make me feel completely OK. And they both thought I should tell my parents what's going on with me. So, I swallowed and took a sip of water, and said, 'Actually, as you're both here, there's something that maybe you should know.'

'What's that, darling?' Mom put on her interested face.

'Go ahead, Ethan.' Dad leaned forward. I leaned back in response.

'It's nothing very important. Just. . . Just. . .'

'Don't be nervous, sweetheart.'

I glared. 'I'm not nervous. I just thought you should know that I split up with my boyfriend. But it's fine because I'd only been seeing him for a couple of weeks, and I'm not into relationships, and I dumped him, so I'm not heartbroken or anything.'

I saw them glance at each other. I ploughed on.

'And I know you think that the point of this is me telling you that I like boys, but it isn't because actually I like girls. And boys. But I don't really like people, so I'm sort of telling you that I could get with anyone but it's never going to mean much.'

Mom tried to grab my hand but I whipped it away.

'Ethan, sweetie, you can't possibly think that we'd disapprove of your sexuality?'

What possessed me to have this conversation in public? The people at the other table were already staring at Mom anyway, dazzled by her glamour and the way she manages to look like an angel that's fallen to earth, even when she isn't up to her neck in refugee children. When they heard her say that word – slowly, like she was eating it – sex-u-al-ity, they abandoned all pretence of having a conversation of their own.

'It's so common,' said Dad, 'for someone your age to experience confusion about these things. Often it can take a bit of time to work out where your preferences lie. It's not something to feel bad about—'

'I don't feel bad about it—'

'It's just a phase—'

'It's not a *phase*. This is how I am. I'm not asking for your approval.'

'Ethan, honey, of course Dad and I don't disapprove.'

'I suppose you think it's a *phase* as well.'

She smiled. She opened her mouth. I knew, just before she spoke, exactly what she was going to say.

'Ethan, honey, I've known people who had to flee for their lives just because they were homosexual. People whose families informed on them to the ayatollahs or the Taliban, people who'd been tortured, maimed, whipped. . .'

'Steady on, Melinda.' Dad had clearly forgotten what she could be like.

'Boys just older than you, running away from certain death, having seen their partners murdered for the supposed sin of loving another man. I mean I'm happy for you, darling, that this is not an issue for you. You live in one of the most liberal cities in the world. You can do exactly what you like and no one will persecute you for it.'

'So you don't think it's a *phase*? Or you do?'

'For some people bisexuality is a stage in their journey to homosexuality. For others –' she shrugged – 'it's the way they are. But aren't you lucky that really it doesn't matter one way or another?'

'Yeah,' I said. 'Lucky me.'

'You do take precautions, don't you?' Dad's voice is softer than Mom's but it carried at least as far as the waitress, who was hovering to clear our table but changed her mind and backtracked to the kitchen.

'Yeah, yeah, right, whatever, actually my business,' I muttered into my plate. Was he utterly stupid? Mom's been giving me lectures about STDs since I was seven years old.

'I've made sure Ethan knows the facts of life,' she informed him now.

'I didn't mean to offend you, Ethan,' said Dad.

'Well, can you just leave it, please? I just thought you might want to know.' I couldn't quite remember what had made me embark on this mad and stupid path, but I was highly regretting it. I didn't feel better at all – in fact I felt a million times worse. And I couldn't work out why, because all that had happened was that I'd told them something that only made me happy. When you find people difficult, like I do, it's a very positive thing to find men and women attractive. It doubles your chances of finding someone to hang out with and do fun things, including having sex. And sex, so far, is the best thing I've found to do with someone else – much better than talking or dating and all that sharing crap.

'We did want to know, sweetheart.' Mom beamed at me. 'You did the right thing in telling us.'

'We only want to help and support you,' Dad chimed in. 'You know you can bring any problems to us.'

'I don't have problems,' I growled. 'Except Mom not agreeing to the Airbnb thing. That's a problem.'

'Why did you break up with your boyfriend?' asked Mom. 'Tell us about him, darling. Are you sure you're not upset?'

'On a scale of one to ten, ten being getting crucified by the Taliban, I'd say breaking up with Tim scores about zero point. . .' I couldn't remember if it made the number bigger or smaller if I added in a lot more zeros. 'Zero point one. That's all.'

'That's quite a lot,' said Dad.

'No it isn't.' Annoyingly I seemed to have something in my eye. I dropped my head, letting my hair fall over my face, and blinked it away.

'What happened?'

'Oh, nothing. He just . . . he wanted more than I wanted, because I don't do relationships, that is, not like he wanted, so I wasn't going to get into something heavy, you know, love and all that crap, that's not me, even Rosa who I really love, it's as a friend, even when we do sleep together, because Rosa, she's never going to want just one guy and even if she did it wouldn't be me, we're just friends with benefits, and that's absolutely fine by me.'

Silence. I kept my head down. Who'd have known there were so many words inside me?

The waitress cleared the table, sweeping up the little bits of coconut, the stray peanuts, the grains of yellow rice, so the tablecloth was clean and tidy once again. Mom and Dad consulted the dessert menu, Mom explaining the options – stripy *spekkoek*, jackfruit, banana fritters. I looked at my lap, and breathed and wished I'd never started this whole thing, this conversation which had left me so broken when there was nothing at all to be broken about.

Mom ordered jackfruit for me because that's what I always have, chewy jackfruit and pineapple sorbet and little glowing kumquats. Dad left the table, going off to find the bathroom.

'I'm going to miss you,' said Mum, voice low and gentle.

I didn't reply. Mom and me missing each other is the ultimate first world problem.

'It's OK, you know. We're very happy that you trusted us with this.'

I sighed. She didn't get it. She didn't get me. Neither of them ever have.

Dad came back. I could smell soap. I could tell that his hands would feel damp and cold.

'Look, this is no big deal,' I told them. 'I mean it. I couldn't care less what you think about this.'

Goldfish faces.

'But there is something I never told you. And maybe I should, because when you say stuff like. . .' My throat tightened, so it was hard to swallow. 'Like, you're confused, you don't know how you feel, what you want. . .'

'I didn't mean—' Dad floundered.

I carried on. 'It makes me remember when you made me decide how I felt. When I had to make a choice. And I never felt so bad in my life.'

I was nine. I was a skinny little kid with a pale face and dark shadows under his eyes, and no friends. And I was all alone with this guy in a room full of dark furniture – an older man, with a wig in a box on the table.

It was grey and sort of frizzy, but in a controlled way. And when he saw me looking at it, he took it out of the box and let me touch it and explained that it was made of horsehair, that people wore wigs like it all the time hundreds of years ago, that in court he had to wear it, but when he talked to little boys like me he took it off.

'Why do you have to wear it?' I asked him.

'Tradition,' he told me.

It was the weirdest thing ever.

And then he asked the question. The Question. Who did I want to live with, Mom or Dad?

'Can't I live with both of them?' I asked the judge man. 'Can't you stop Mom taking me off to places, and we can just live together, in a house, a proper house?'

'I could make an order keeping you in England,' said the judge, 'but then your mother would not be able to take you to live in Amsterdam as she wants.'

'If I had to stay in England, could she do her work?'

'She could, but she would have to leave you behind.'

'And would I have to live with Dad and his friend?'

'What would you like?'

I didn't like Dad's girlfriend. He hadn't met Sandra yet. This one was called Celia and she had a noisy dog, and she smelled sour and wore sunglasses which made her look like a beetle.

'Mom,' I said. Then, 'But not going to scary places.'

The judge wrote something down, and immediately I was terrified. That Dad would find out and hate me. That Mom would never go anywhere she wanted again and hate me too. That I would be responsible for refugees starving and Dad feeling sad and the world ending.

'Don't tell them, don't tell them!' I said in a panic.

The judge handed me a tissue and a metal box.

'Take a look in there,' he said.

I looked. The box was full of candy. I took a handful.

'I won't tell them,' he said. 'Don't worry.'

Now, I took a spoonful of pineapple sorbet, and it burned its way down my throat.

'We thought it was for the best,' said Mom, crumbling her *spekkoek*.

'You were always so grown up,' said Dad. 'And we couldn't agree.'

'We're sorry,' said Mom. 'Divorce is never easy.'

'We're sorry,' said Dad. 'We should have done a better job of working things out.'

I breathed. And I chewed jackfruit, and I thought about skating in the Vondelpark and painting the spare bathroom, and maybe calling up Tim – maybe losing myself in his arms again, giving myself another dose of his soft hair, his brown eyes. Or, if not Tim, then perhaps someone else. Maybe I wasn't so worthless after all.

'It's OK,' I said.

And then.

'So can I do the Airbnb thing? When I'm eighteen?'

ABOUT THE AUTHORS

BRYONY PEARCE

Bryony lives in the Forest of Dean and is a full-time mum to her two children, husband and various pets. She is vegetarian and loves chocolate, wine and writing. People are often surprised at how dark her writing is, as she is generally pretty nice. When the children let her off taxi duty and out of the house, she enjoys doing school visits, festivals and events.

Her novels for young adults include: *Angel's Fury* (a dark thriller about a teenage girl who has been reincarnated), *The Weight of Souls* (a supernatural thriller about a teenage girl who sees dead people), *Phoenix Rising* and *Phoenix Burning* (dystopian adventures about pirates who sail on a junk-filled sea), *Windrunner's Daughter* (a science-fiction adventure set on Mars) and *Wavefunction* (a science-fiction novel about a boy who can jump between universes).

Website: www.bryonypearce.co.uk
Twitter: @BryonyPearce
Facebook author page: BryonyPearceAuthor
Email: admin@bryonypearce.co.uk

PAULA RAWSTHORNE

Until her thirties, Paula Rawsthorne had no idea that she was a writer. Then she won a national BBC writing competition and her comic tale was read by Bill Nighy on Radio 4. Her dark stories for adults have been published in anthologies of contemporary literature. Her first young adult novel, *The Truth about Celia Frost* was a winner in the Society of Children's Book Writers and Illustrators (SCBWI) Undiscovered Voices competition. Published by Usborne, it was shortlisted for eleven literary awards and won the Leeds Book Award, the Sefton Super Reads and the Nottingham Brilliant Book Award. Her second novel, *Blood Tracks* was also shortlisted for a number of awards and won the Rib Valley Book Award.

Paula's story 'A Foreign Land' was commissioned by Nottingham UNESCO City of Literature and published in *These Seven*. Paula has worked with numerous groups on issues raised by this story about a young asylum seeker.

Paula is invited to do author visits and workshops in secondary schools throughout the country and is a writer in residence for the literacy organisation First Story. She's currently writing her third novel and lives in Nottingham with her husband and three children who are all much taller than her.

Website: www.paularawsthorne.wordpress.com
Twitter: @PaulaRawsthorne
Facebook: PaulaRawsthorneAuthor

DAVE COUSINS

Dave Cousins' books have been hailed as 'teen realism with action, humour and heart'.

Published in over twelve languages across the world, *15 Days without a Head* was a *Sunday Times* Children's Book of the Week, winner of the Premio Andersen in Italy, and the SCBWI Crystal Kite for the UK and Europe. *Waiting for Gonzo* won the Grampian Children's Book Award and has its own original soundtrack album, complete with accompanying music videos! Both books were nominated for the Carnegie Medal. Dave is also the author/illustrator of the Charlie Merrick's Misfits series.

When not creating stories in his attic, Dave travels extensively, visiting schools, libraries and book festivals across the UK and abroad. His events have been described as 'stand-up with books' or, as one year seven student put it, 'Well funny!'

Mina from 'Magpie Soup' first appeared in *15 Days without a Head*. 'She was one of those characters who came alive on the page,' explains Dave. 'I always knew there was more to her story than I was able to put in *15 Days*. . .'Magpie Soup' was a chance to let Mina have her say. I hope you enjoy it.'

'Magpie Soup' originally appeared in the World Book Day app in 2013. This is the first time it has been available in print.

Website: www.davecousins.net
Twitter: @DaveCousins9000
Instagram: @DaveC9000

SARA GRANT

Sara is a writer of multiple personalities! She writes fiction for young adults, teens and young readers. Her stories range from action-adventure in exotic locations to fairy godmothers in training and apocalyptic tales of survival and love. Chasing Danger, her new action-adventure series for teens, is Sara's dream project, combining her love of thrillers, travel and girl power. She imagined the first book as a little bit like *Charlie's Angels* and *Die Hard* on a desert island.

Dark Parties, her first young adult novel, won the SCBWI Crystal Kite Award for Europe. Her next teen novel, *Half Lives*, is a story told in two voices from a pre- and post-apocalyptic time. She also writes a funny magical series for young readers, titled Magic Trix. As a freelance editor of series fiction, she has worked on twelve different series and edited nearly 100 books. She has given writing workshops in the USA, UK and Europe and teaches a master's class on writing for children/teens at Goldsmiths University. She graduated from Indiana University with degrees in journalism and psychology, and later she earned a master's degree in creative and life writing at Goldsmiths College, University of London. She lives in London.

Website: www.sara-grant.com
Twitter: @AuthorSaraGrant

KATIE DALE

Author and actress Katie Dale had her first poem 'The Fate of The School Hamster' published at age eight, and hasn't stopped writing since! She studied English Literature at Sheffield University, followed by a crazy year at drama school, a summer playing Juliet in a national Shakespeare tour, and eight months backpacking through South East Asia – where she learned that she was a winner of the inaugural SCBWI Undiscovered Voices competition, which launched her writing career.

She has written for all ages, including a treasury of bedtime stories for toddlers, a series of rhyming *Fairy Tale Twists* for primary-age children, a middle grade comedy/drama *Mumnesia*, and two young adult novels.

Someone Else's Life, the story of a teenage girl who discovers she was switched at birth, won both the Brilliant Books Award and the Mad About Books Award and is now published all over the world. *Little White Lies* is a psychological thriller about a girl who changes her identity when she goes to university in pursuit of revenge, and won the UKYA bloggers' award for 'Best Ending'.

Katie happily visits schools all over the UK, and as far afield as Moscow!

Website: www.katiedaleuk.blogspot.com
Twitter: @katiedaleuk
Email: katiedaleauthor@hotmail.com

SAVITA KALHAN

Savita Kalhan was born in India but has lived in the UK most of her life. She graduated from Aberystwyth University with a degree in Politics and Philosophy. She was a batik artist before going to live in the Middle East for several years where she taught English and began to write.

Now living in North London, she spends her time writing, playing tennis, growing veg and super-hot chillies on her allotment, and loves to get the boxing gloves on.

Savita is a member of the Scattered Authors Society and blogs regularly at *An Awfully Big Blog Adventure* (http://awfullybigblogadventure.blogspot.co.uk). She runs a teen reading group at her local library in Finchley.

Her novel, *The Long Weekend*, published by Andersen Press, is a tense teen thriller about two boys who are abducted after school. *The Long Weekend* was shortlisted for the Fabulous Book Award 2010. Her short story, 'The Poet' was published in the short story anthology, *Even Birds are Chained to the Sky*.

Website: www.savitakalhan.com
Twitter: @savitakalhan

MIRIAM HALAHMY

Miriam Halahmy lives in London near Hampstead Heath and is married with two grown-up children and one grandson who is teaching her how to swing through trees again. Miriam loves to write in cafes all over the world and finds the hiss of the coffee machine a great inspiration. When Miriam is not writing she loves reading, theatre and travel. She collects oceans – four so far – and isn't shy in any foreign language.

Miriam writes novels, poems and short stories for children, teens and adults. Her YA novel *Hidden* (in which two teens rescue an asylum seeker from the sea and hide him to save him from being deported) was a *Sunday Times* Children's Book of the Week and nominated for the Carnegie Medal. It is currently being adapted for the stage and will be published in America in 2016.

Hidden was followed by two more YA novels: *Illegal* – about a girl who is forced to courier drugs and struggles to free herself from the criminals, and *Stuffed* – a love story about two teens who are each hiding a terrible secret from the other.

Miriam's new novel, *The Emergency Zoo* (Alma Books, May 2016) is for 8-12 year-olds and tells an untold Second World War story about domestic pets and their terrible fate.

Website: www.miriamhalahmy.com
Twitter: @miriamhalahmy
Facebook author page: Miriam Halahmy – Writer

KEREN DAVID

Keren David was apprenticed as a reporter on a national newspaper at the age of nineteen and was an assistant news editor at *The Independent* eight years later. She moved to Amsterdam in 1999 and worked as editor in chief of a photojournalism agency. On her return to London in 2007 she started writing her first young adult book, *When I was Joe*, which was published in 2010.

When I Was Joe was nominated for the Carnegie Medal, shortlisted for the Branford Boase award and the UKLA award, and highly commended for the Teenage Booktrust Prize. It won five regional awards and was shortlisted for six more. It was followed by two sequels, *Almost True* (2010) and *Another Life* (2012).

Keren's book *Lia's Guide to Winning the Lottery* (2011) was also nominated for the Carnegie medal, and was one of *Kirkus*'s Best Teen Reads for 2012. Keren is adapting it as a musical with composer Paul Herbert and lyricist Lesley Ross.

Salvage (2014) was shortlisted for the *Bookseller*'s YA Prize, and also for the YA section of the Romantic Novel of the Year. It was nominated for the Carnegie Medal and shortlisted for seven regional awards.

Keren's latest book is *This is Not a Love Story*, which has been long-listed for the UKLA book award and nominated for the Carnegie Medal. Keren's short story 'The Day I Told the Truth' is a prequel to *This is Not a Love Story*. Keren says, 'Ethan, who narrates the short story, doesn't get to have his say in the book, and it was a joy to give him his own story. To fit in with the timeline of the book, I've slightly altered the timing of the annual Amsterdam Pride parade – sorry! – by shunting it a few months earlier.'

Website: www.kerendavid.com

A WORD OF THANKS ...

Writing is often a solitary occupation. One of the reasons we formed The Edge was to break away from that solitude and join forces to share our passion for great stories. In the five years since The Edge began we have received wonderful encouragement from many like-minded people. We would like to express our heartfelt appreciation to the many librarians, teachers, booksellers, bloggers and journalists for their support, with special thanks to Matt Imrie and Sue Shaper.

Taking stories to readers requires a long chain of dedicated people, and we would like to thank the following for helping us take this anthology from a vague idea scribbled on the back of a train ticket to an actual book! Jenny Savill at Andrew Nurnberg Associates; Karen Ball and Sarah Castleton at Atom; Anne Clark Literary Agency; Sarah Manson; Jasmine Richards at OUP; and Clare Conville at Conville and Walsh. A special mention for Dean Valley Primary School, whose Internet safety day scared Bryony 'half to death' and made her want to write the story that opens this anthology.

To our editor, Maurice Lyon, for his word wrangling wisdom, enthusiasm and time; to Emily Sharratt for her support and for casting a professional eye over the manuscript and making sure all our 'i's are dotted and our 't's are crossed; to everyone at Albury Books for their enthusiasm for the project, especially Hannah and En; and to Joy Court, for being kind enough to write our introduction and champion The Edge from day one – we salute you!

Thanks to our families and all those who have supported our writing careers over the years, and finally . . . we would like to thank you, the reader – without whom these stories would remain incomplete. We hope you enjoy them.

The Edge, Summer 2016